"I think you're amazing."

Molly's heartbeat picked up. "I think you're amazing, too."

Unbuckling his seat belt, Bret turned to her. "That's nice to hear. And if you were planning to establish a life for yourself in Wagon Train—"

"Which doesn't seem likely." In the faint light from the dash, his eyes were more gray than blue. Still mesmerizing, though. She took a breath. "You're looking for someone for the long haul."

"Yes, ma'am." His tone was low, sexy.

It sent shivers through her. "Me, too."

"Keeping your promise."

"Yes." Her gaze drifted to his lips. Chiseled. Tempting. "So the smart thing...."

"Would be to put a lid on this."

She couldn't resist asking, just to see what he'd say. "*This?*" She unfastened her seatbelt so she could face him.

"What's happening between us."

"So far that's nothing." Not quite true. Her body hummed with awareness. She had no business prolonging the exchange, but it was so delicious.

His eyes darkened. "So far."

ROCKING THE COWBOY'S CHRISTMAS

ROWDY RANCH

Vicki Lewis Thompson

Ocean Dance Press

ROCKING THE COWBOY'S CHRISTMAS

ISBN: 978-1-63803-941-9

Ocean Dance Press LLC
PO Box 69901
Oro Valley, AZ 85737

Visit the author's website at
VickiLewisThompson.com

Want more cowboys? Check out these other titles by Vicki Lewis Thompson

Rowdy Ranch

Having the Cowboy's Baby
Stoking the Cowboy's Fire
Testing the Cowboy's Resolve
Rocking the Cowboy's Christmas

The Buckskin Brotherhood

Sweet-Talking Cowboy
Big-Hearted Cowboy
Baby-Daddy Cowboy
True-Blue Cowboy
Strong-Willed Cowboy
Secret-Santa Cowboy
Stand-Up Cowboy
Single-Dad Cowboy
Marriage-Minded Cowboy
Gift-Giving Cowboy

The McGavin Brothers

A Cowboy's Strength
A Cowboy's Honor
A Cowboy's Return
A Cowboy's Heart
A Cowboy's Courage
A Cowboy's Christmas
A Cowboy's Kiss
A Cowboy's Luck
A Cowboy's Charm
A Cowboy's Challenge
A Cowboy's Baby

A Cowboy's Holiday
A Cowboy's Choice
A Cowboy's Worth
A Cowboy's Destiny
A Cowboy's Secret
A Cowboy's Homecoming

Sons of Chance
What a Cowboy Wants
A Cowboy's Temptation
Claimed by the Cowboy
Should've Been a Cowboy
Cowboy Up
Cowboys Like Us
It's Christmas, Cowboy
Count on a Cowboy
The Way to a Cowboy's Heart
Trust in a Cowboy
Only a Cowboy Will Do
Wild About the Cowboy
Cowboys and Angels

1

Twenty luminarias. As the Canadian Brass blared Christmas carols in the background, Bret McLintock put the finishing touches on number fifteen and shut down the torch. He glanced at the clock. Almost six.

His passion was forge welding, the historic choice, but this order on a short timeframe required him to be nimble and speedy. He'd resorted to the torch. If he kept up a steady pace, he might finish by nine, assuming he didn't stop for dinner. His stomach rumbled.

He should have agreed to make ten instead of twenty, especially this close to Christmas. Gil, his younger brother and business partner, had said as much. But the customer had come up with the idea at the last minute and had a party planned for Saturday, one week before Christmas.

Gil had gallantly offered to help complete the last-minute order. But he would have had to cancel his plan to take his date for a sleighride out at the ranch. Bret wasn't about to let his brother make that sacrifice because his idiot sibling had bitten off more than he could chew.

And speaking of chewing, a burger from the Fluffy Buffalo would go good right now. Since he and Gil had rented this storefront in town back in October, that option was open to him. But if he took a break, he'd be tempted to order a beer and settle into the festive mood at the Buffalo.

Wiping his forehead on his sleeve, he took a few swallows from his water jug and picked up the torch. Before he could turn it on, his phone chimed. A number he didn't recognize rolled across the top of the screen. Likely a nuisance call.

He put down the torch and grabbed the phone anyway. Gil teased him about his habit of doing that. *Let it ring, bro. If it's important, they'll leave a message.* "McLintock Metalworks. How can I help you?"

"Hey, Bret, it's Jerry over at the tree lot. I noticed your truck was still there."

"Finishing up a project I promised to get done before tomorrow morning."

"Oh, then never mind."

"What's up, Jerry?" The tree lot owner was a good guy who wouldn't call unless he had an issue.

"I have a customer who—excuse me a minute." He broke off and had an animated discussion with a woman.

Bret couldn't catch all of it, but clearly the customer hadn't wanted him to make the call.

Jerry came back on the line. "She says she's fine with a small tree, but you should have seen her face when she found the one she really wants. The thing is, it won't fit in her itty-bitty car."

"Sell her the big one. I'll be over with my truck."

"I was hoping you'd say that. This is her first Christmas in Montana. She should have the tree she wants."

"Definitely. I'll see you in ten minutes." Taking off his goggles and apron, he shut everything down before grabbing his keys, his jacket and his hat. He wouldn't finish by nine. Oh, well.

A light snow coated the windshield but a quick swipe with the blades took care of it. The snow had stopped for now. He backed out, made a tight turn and pulled onto the tree lot across the street.

Strands of lights created a canopy over the rows of trees and Dolly Parton's *Hard Candy Christmas* poured from the speaker mounted near the entrance. Bret had no trouble spotting the woman's car, a light blue compact in a row of pickups and SUVs. Hardly anyone drove something that small in Wagon Train.

She stood beside it, bundled up in a trench coat, red knit hat and a matching scarf. Couldn't tell much about her except that she was trim and short. Several trees leaned against the fence ready to be loaded. He parked near the fence.

Jerry had his hands full with other customers, so Bret headed for the woman. She watched his approach. Her soft brown eyes fringed with dark lashes were pretty, but that wasn't what caught his attention. Although she looked to be about twenty-five, her steady gaze had the depth of someone older, as if she'd been through tough times.

"I'm so sorry, Mr. McLintock." Her mellow voice had an underlying firmness. "I told Jerry the other tree would be fine, but he insisted—"

"I'm more than happy to help, ma'am." He tipped his hat. "I'm Bret."

"Jerry told me. Nice to meet you." She stuck out a gloved hand. "My grammy admires your family a lot."

He grasped her hand. Strong grip. "She lives here?"

"She does. Elvira Johannesen."

"Mrs. J? Used to be the town librarian?"

"Uh-huh. I'm Molly, by the way. Molly Dixon."

"Pleased to meet you, Miss Molly." He liked the way her lips moved when she said her name. She had a very kissable mouth. Probably shouldn't be thinking such things, but she had to be single. Any guy worth his salt would be here to help. "Which tree is yours?"

"The one right by the gate. I was lucky to find such a good one this late in the game. I kept meaning to get over here and suddenly it was December fourteenth."

He glanced at the tree, a nine-footer, at least. Closer to ten. "Beautiful spruce. Needs a high ceiling, though."

"Grammy's parlor ceiling is thirteen feet."

"So it is. I remember that parlor. A lot of bookshelves. Really nice room."

"That's one reason I fell in love with such a tall tree. It'll look amazing in there."

"No question about that." He looked over at her car.

"I know what you're thinking."

He turned back, couldn't help smiling at her rueful expression. "That you had gumption?"

"That's one way to describe it. I was never going to stuff it in my tiny car. I thought maybe I could tie it on the roof, but—"

"Jerry wouldn't go for that in a million years."

Her eyes sparkled when she laughed. "I told him it wasn't far and I'd creep down the street, but he refused to help me tie it on. Said I'd be an accident waiting to happen."

He dismissed the tug of attraction. She was likely just visiting her grandmother for the holidays. "He was right. But I admire your spirit. And your taste in trees. I'll go fetch it." He started toward the gate.

She followed. "I'll pay you for your trouble, of course."

Pausing, he turned back. "That won't be necessary."

"But—"

"Jerry said this is your first Christmas in Wagon Train."

"Yes, but that's no reason—"

"Around here we do favors for each other all the time." He held her gaze. "I'm happy to do one for Mrs. J's granddaughter." Those brown eyes were gorgeous. A man could lose himself in no time.

Her brow puckered. "Did I insult you just now?"

"No insult taken. I'm guessing you're not from a small town."

"Denver."

"Not small."

"Nope. It's a friendly place, but I still would expect to pay a stranger who's hauling my Christmas tree to my house. Or, in this case, Grammy's house."

"Speaking of that, does your grandmother have a stand that can handle a tree this size?"

"That's what inspired me to look for a large one. I found a beautiful old iron stand tucked away with the ornaments. Grammy hasn't used it since Grandpa died, but obviously he made it for a tree like this."

"Can't wait to see it. He did outstanding work."

"You knew him?"

"Sure did. I assume the stand's set up where you want the tree?"

"It is, but you don't have to bring it in. I'm stronger than I look."

"That I believe, but it's part of the service."

She blinked. Then she smiled. "You're a charmer, Bret McLintock."

Backatcha, lady. "Do we have a deal?"

"Yes, we do. Let me call Grammy and alert her."

"I'm not planning to stay. I have—"

"Work to do. I gathered that, so we won't keep you." She pulled her phone from her pocket.

"But if she knows a McLintock is coming to the house, she'll want to put on lipstick."

That amused him. "Okay, then. I'll go grab the tree."

"Great. Thanks."

Bret gave Jerry a wave as he walked over to his truck, put down the tailgate and grabbed his gloves from the cab. Returning to the tree, he grasped the thick trunk with one hand and thumped it on the ground to knock off any loose needles.

Heavy sucker. Smelled great. He checked on Molly of the big brown eyes and kissable mouth. She was still on the phone with her grandmother. She gave him a thumbs-up to let him know he had the right tree.

His evening had taken an interesting turn. He'd get a kick out of seeing Mrs. J again, with lipstick or without. She'd run a tight ship, insisting that kids use their quiet voices. Her replacement wasn't big on that. He didn't drop by the library so much anymore now that the hushed atmosphere was gone.

Too bad Mrs. J's granddaughter was only here for the holidays. Her smile gave him a fizzy sensation in his chest. But if she lived in Denver, he might as well deliver the tree and call it good. He wasn't a holiday fling kind of guy.

2

"Grammy, is Zach asleep?" Molly kept her voice down so Bret wouldn't hear the conversation. He probably couldn't from this distance, but she wanted to play it safe.

"Zach's out like a light. Did you find a tree?"

"I did." She was distracted by Bret as he hoisted the large evergreen to his shoulder like it was a broom. Then he turned and started toward his truck.

She'd never been an ogler, but... oh, my. His waist-length leather jacket provided a fabulous view of his tight buns in action.

Surprise, surprise, she got a little damp and achy. Hallelujah, she wasn't dead inside. Thank goodness.

"What kind did you get?"

Kind? What was Grammy talking about? Oh. The tree. "Um, blue spruce. It's... spectacular."

"Have you been running? You sound out of breath."

"It's probably the cold air." Or the hot cowboy.

"Dinner will be ready in about fifteen minutes. We can decorate the tree after we eat."

"Sounds perfect. The thing is, the tree's too big for my car, so—"

"Jerry's bringing it? He's such a sweetie."

"He is a sweetie, but he's too busy with customers to bring it. Bret McLintock offered."

"No kidding? That's marvelous!"

"He's loading it in his pickup right now." A lustrous cobalt blue beauty. No boring colors for this guy.

"I've always liked that boy."

Boy? Grammy needed new glasses.

"How did he get into the picture?"

"Jerry called his shop and asked him to help me. I'm sure he was in the middle of a project, but he came right over, anyway."

"Of course he did. He's a McLintock."

"He also insists on carrying it into the house, so you'll need to hide Zach's toys."

"I'm on it."

"I told him I had to call so you'd have a chance to put on lipstick."

"Did you, now?" Her grandmother chuckled. "Guess I have to slap some on, then. Hate that stuff."

"Sorry. It was the only excuse I could think of."

"It's fine. In fact, it's serendipitous. Right out of the box, you've found yourself a highly eligible McLintock. Invite him to dinner."

She gasped and turned away to shield her reaction. "Are you nuts?"

"I prefer the word eccentric."

"What if Zach wakes up?"

"I'll say I'm babysitting for a friend. Which is true."

"It's too big a risk."

"In case you haven't heard, the way to a man's heart is through his stomach."

"I just met him ten minutes ago. I'm not looking for a way to his heart. Or any other part of his anatomy."

"My spidey senses are tingling, Molly. If you won't invite him to dinner, I will."

"You're playing with fire."

"I know. Isn't it fun?"

"*No.* Just let him bring the tree in and head on back to his shop, okay? He has work to do."

"We'll see how it goes, honey. Bye." She disconnected.

Molly groaned. Her grandmother's response wasn't a surprise. She couldn't wait for Molly to find a lovely new husband. But they'd agreed Zach should remain a secret in this town until Mr. Right showed up and proved himself worthy.

Inviting Bret to dinner could blow the plan to smithereens. Or not. Her son was a sound sleeper, especially in a quiet house instead of the noisy apartment complex they'd lived in until three weeks ago.

Enough dithering. Bret must wonder why she'd stayed on the phone so long.

Sure enough, when she turned around, he was leaning against the back fender of his truck, arms crossed over his broad chest, his attention focused on her. Making eye contact sent a quiver through her stomach.

Pushing away from the fender, he sauntered in her direction. "Long call for a lipstick alert."

"It turned into more than that. She's invited you to dinner."

"Oh?"

"I warned her you'd been working when Jerry called and you might not—"

"Dinner sounds great."

"Alrighty, then." She couldn't decide if his eyes were blue or green. She needed more time to study them. Like over a glass of wine. Next to a crackling fire. Clearly her worry that she'd lost interest in men was unfounded.

"I haven't talked with your grandmother in ages. Not since the funeral." He paused. "Were you there? If you were, I don't—"

"I didn't make it. It was sudden." The image of wine and a cozy fire evaporated. "I was... on my honeymoon."

"You're married?" A flicker of surprise.

"I was. He...um...died last year. In October."

He winced. "I'm so sorry."

"It hasn't been easy. Last Christmas was awful, so I'm determined this one will be better."

"The tree means more than I realized."

His empathy smoothed the ripple of sadness. "It means a lot to me, for sure, and probably for my grandmother, too. Thank you for hauling it for us."

"I'm happy to do it."

"You know the way?"

"I do, but I'll wait until you pull out and follow you over."

"Okay." What a likeable guy.

"See you in a few." He tipped his hat.

Ooo, nice. The wine and cozy fire scenario slipped back into focus. No wonder women fantasized about cowboys. Hurrying to her car, she hopped in, started it up and backed out of her parking space.

She'd tuned her radio to the local country station and an instrumental version of *Silent Night* played as she drove slowly down Main Street. Growing up in Boston and living in Denver for several years, she was used to lavish holiday displays.

Wagon Train didn't need that. The small town was already a postcard. Add sparkling lights, handmade window decorations, wreaths on every door and red bows on the lamp posts and you had a nostalgic image as warm as a hug, and as sweet as a kiss under the mistletoe.

She'd arrived for Thanksgiving, and ever since she'd absorbed every drop of Christmas spirit in this lovely small town. A year ago she'd been a grieving, pregnant widow who wasn't cleared to fly, which kept her from spending the holidays with her parents and in-laws in Boston.

A massive East Coast storm had kept her folks from coming to Denver until after New Year's

Eve. Her friends had rallied in the meantime, but they'd been fighting impossible odds.

This holiday she had her incredible child and a temporary home with Grammy, who'd admitted she needed them as much as they needed her. To top it off, a handsome cowboy had offered to transport the most beautiful tree on the lot to Grammy's house.

The grille of his massive truck hovered in her rearview mirror and her heartrate picked up every time she glanced at it. She wouldn't admit that to her grandmother. The woman had already decided Bret's sudden appearance was Meant to Be.

Putting on her turn signal, she pulled into the driveway of Grammy's classic Victorian, a storybook house with original gingerbread trim. It looked festive even without Christmas decorations, and fabulous with them.

Last week she and Grammy had strung lights on the porch railing and hung a fragrant pine wreath on the front door. Electric candles glowed in the windows, both upstairs and down.

Molly and Zach's presence had lit a spark, and Grammy had brought down boxes of decorations from the attic. Mesmerized, Zach had made cooing noises as a charming array of sleighs, reindeer, Santas and even an illuminated Christmas village had appeared.

A gorgeous tree in the parlor would add the finishing touch. She climbed out of her car and walked to the curb as Bret pulled up. She met him by the tailgate.

Lowering it, he flashed her a smile. "The place sure looks nice."

"Thanks. We've had fun decorating."

"Coming here brings back memories of the blacksmith shop behind the house. Is it still there?" He tugged on a pair of work gloves.

"Yes, but it's boarded up. You paid a visit to Grandpa?"

"Yes, ma'am. After Gil and I completed our farrier's course, we asked for his advice on opening our business. He gave us some great tips that kept us from making rookie mistakes."

"That sounds like Grandpa Hank. He loved passing on his knowledge."

"He did more than that. He contacted his former clients and gave us a recommendation. That was trusting, considering he didn't know if we were any good."

"Except you and your brother are McLintocks. According to my grandmother, that counts for a great deal in this town."

"I credit my mom on that score."

She added modesty to the growing list of Bret's admirable traits. "Credit yourself, too. As Grammy says, it's not just the brand, it's the folks who wear it."

"She did say that. It'll be good to see her again. It's been too long." He reached in, dragged out the tree and balanced it on his shoulder. "Close that for me, please?"

"Sure." She pushed it shut. "Pretty truck."

"Thanks. Gil tried to talk me into tan or white — our magnetic logo stands out more on a lighter color." He headed toward the shoveled walk leading to the porch. "But that blue caught my eye."

"Mine, too." Women were probably lined up waiting for a ride in Bret's cobalt blue truck. Or maybe one special lady had already claimed the passenger seat. Molly skirted around him and scampered up the steps so she could get the door.

Her grandmother beat her to the punch, propping it open. She'd put on the requisite lipstick. "What a beauty, Bret! A tree like that hasn't come into this house in years. Thank you."

"My pleasure, Mrs. J. Something sure smells good."

"Chicken and dumplings."

"Seriously? With corn bread?"

"What else?"

"We had that all the time when I was a kid. Not so much anymore. Mom says it's fattening, but it's one of my favorites."

"I hope that means you're staying."

"I wouldn't miss it. This goes in the parlor, right?"

"Yes, please." She closed the door and gestured to a room on the left.

"It'll look good in there." He headed for the doorway.

Grammy lowered her voice. "Talk about looking good. That boy's filled out since I last saw him."

"Oh? He wasn't always—"

"Ripped?"

Molly stifled a giggle.

"What, you think I don't know that word?"

"I'm convinced you know every word in the dictionary and even more that aren't. I've just never heard you use that one."

"Because I haven't had the occasion. Now skedaddle in there and help that handsome man with the tree while I see about dinner." She made a beeline for the kitchen. Evidently Bret had her stamp of approval.

Taking off her hat, scarf and trench coat, Molly left them on the coat rack in the entry and walked into the parlor. Grammy wasn't wrong. Bret had the muscles of a lumberjack and the arresting gaze of a movie star. Green eyes or blue? A blend?

He'd lowered the tree into the stand and was holding it steady, his hat nudged back. "Just in time, Miss Molly. Tell me if it's straight."

Centering herself in front of it, she eyed both tree and cowboy. "Perfect."

"Would you mind crawling under there and tightening the bolts while I hold it?"

"Be happy to." The familiar routine gave her a twinge of sadness because it wasn't Aaron keeping the tree in place while she secured it in the stand. But a twinge was a vast improvement over the waves of grief that had marked last year's holiday.

It helped that Bret looked nothing like Aaron. Her late husband had been a cotton slacks and oxford-shirt-wearing elementary school teacher, slight of build and fond of golf.

There was nothing slight about this cowboy and she doubted he'd ever set foot on a golf course. As she screwed in the bolts, she had a view of scuffed boots that had to be at least a size twelve and muscular calves that stretched the wear-softened denim of his jeans.

Evergreen branches blocked the rest of him. Well, not quite. A break in the foliage perfectly framed his… no, she shouldn't look. But she did. Lord Almighty. He certainly gave a girl something to think about.

Thank goodness her hormones hadn't taken a permanent vacay. That was fortunate. She and Aaron had been only children, and she'd promised him that Zach would have a baby brother or sister. Providing Zach with a sibling would require that she—

"Can I let go, yet?"

"Almost!" She turned the last bolt once more. "That should do it."

"Let's see if it wobbles. Nope. Good job."

She backed out.

"Let me help you up."

She lifted her head and her attention snagged right where it shouldn't have, which made her blush.

He extended his hand. The gloves were gone, likely stuffed in his coat pocket. She grabbed onto him. Steady grip. Warm. She met his gaze as he hauled her to her feet. Her breath caught. She went still, spellbound by the flare of interest in his incredible eyes.

His fingers closed more securely around hers, heating her from head to toe. What was going on? She'd never been instantly attracted to a man in her life.

Whatever was happening, he was in the same boat. There was no mistaking the way his pupils dilated and his nostrils flared.

She swallowed. "Thanks."

"You're welcome, Miss Molly." He slowly released her hand.

"You must be roasting in that jacket."

"Didn't notice." Breaking eye contact, he shrugged out of it and took off his hat. "How long are you here for?"

Leading question. Yep, he was interested. "I... I don't know."

His eyebrows lifted. "Don't you have to go back to Denver?"

"No, I— oh, I'll bet you thought I was just visiting."

"Yes, ma'am, I surely did." He smiled, clearly happy to be wrong.

"We've—I mean, *I've* moved here. For now, anyway. I lost my job and Grammy's generously invited me to stay with her while I look for another one."

"I'm sorry about the job, but... I'm glad you're staying for a while."

"Me, too." She resisted the urge to look into his captivating eyes. Time to tap on the brakes and slow this thing down. "Let's hang up your coat and check on dinner."

3

Bret got his hopes up that Molly might stick around, but they were squashed flat during dinner. She was in hotel management. She wouldn't find the job she was looking for in Wagon Train.

She'd sent her resume out to several promising locations. Business in the industry was picking up, but given the holidays, she didn't expect to hear back until after New Year's. She had high hopes that at least one would offer her a job. Given that, he'd best steer clear.

Wouldn't be easy. Whenever he glanced across the table and discovered those brown eyes focused on him, lightning shot through his veins. His fingers itched to touch the glossy hair that fell in waves to the shoulders of her red sweater.

Eating a meal across the table from a woman with a kissable mouth could be fun if a guy had the prospect of doing something about those urges after they'd both left the table. But he'd be insane to kiss Molly. He liked everything about her, and one kiss would lead to... yes, it would.

His response confused the hell out of him. Sure, she was pretty, but he'd met plenty of good-looking women in the years since he'd started growing chest hair.

Maybe it was her voice. She pitched it lower than a lot of ladies he'd met. Her laughter had a sultry quality that jacked up his pulse. *I'll bet she'd be fun in bed.* Whoa, Bessie! Where had that highly inappropriate notion come from?

Good thing nobody at this table could read his mind. Mrs. J had picked up on his preoccupation with her granddaughter, though. Her sly wink a while ago had told him as much.

Just like in the old days, Mrs. J didn't miss a trick. Hadn't aged much in five years except her short hair was white instead of gray and she had a few more smile lines.

She'd been smiling a lot during the meal because he'd laid on the compliments about the food. He'd meant every word. Talking up the hearty chicken and dumplings and the tasty cornbread had distracted him from his growing obsession with Molly.

Or maybe he'd made it worse. Good food and good sex were his two favorite things. He had a healthy appetite for both. When Mrs. J brought out a chocolate cake for dessert, she cut him an extra-large slice. Oh, yeah, she had his number.

He had hers, too. Her great food was seasoned with ulterior motives. She would love for this chance encounter at the tree lot to spark a romance. Naturally she'd want her granddaughter to find happiness. If she fell for a local boy, maybe she'd even stay in Wagon Train.

It was a long shot. Molly's career was best pursued in a highly populated area like Denver. A conglomerate had bought the boutique hotel she'd managed and installed its own people. She hadn't found anything else in Denver that suited her, but she would eventually hire on at a similar place.

"I couldn't have worked for that company." Molly forked up the last bite of her cake. "Even if they'd wanted to keep me, I'd have turned them down."

That intrigued him. Being out of a job was no picnic. That was why he and Gil were in business for themselves. "How come?"

She paused, her fork in the air. "They're concentrating on short-term profit. They cut our complimentary fireplace happy hour, saying it wasn't cost effective. But it brought us so much return business that I'm sure it paid for itself." She popped the cake in her mouth.

"They didn't consider that?"

"They demanded supportive data, and I'd never collected any. But I know people came back because of that tradition. I loved it, too. Mingling with everyone before I went home was my favorite part of the job."

"You and my brother Gil would get along. He loves the craft fairs where he can meet with folks who might become customers." He sighed. "Whereas I… I'm not a fan."

"Why not?" Picking up her coffee cup, she took a sip.

"I'm not good at trying to convince someone to buy what I've made. Gil's great at it, so mostly I just stand around doing nothing while he talks us up. I'd rather be in the shop creating."

"What if you created during the fair?"

He frowned. "I'm not sure how that would work."

"It could be like a program we had at the hotel. We booked local artists and designated a part of our lobby as their temporary studio. We had painters, sculptors, writers, musicians. Maybe if you worked on something during the event, you'd enjoy—"

"Welding in that space would be a challenge, and putting on a performance..." He shuddered. "Kill me now." Whoops. He'd just rejected her attempt to be helpful. "Sorry, that was rude."

"Not really. Just honest."

"Being in the spotlight is my least favorite thing. It messes with my concentration."

"Because you're a solitary artist." Mrs. J jumped into the conversation. "You need to be alone with your project. That's when the magic happens."

He glanced at her. "That's nice of you to say, but I don't consider myself an artist."

"But a while ago you called Hank's tree stand a work of art."

"Which it is. I've never made one, but after seeing his, I want to play around with some designs, variations on what he did. Knowing he did it using a forge and hammers impresses the heck out of me. I've gotta try it."

"That's art," Molly said.

"That's imitation. His original concept is artistic, but I'd just be building on it."

"Bret." Mrs. J eyed him the same way she used to fifteen years ago, pinning him in place with a stern gaze framed by her tortoise-shell glasses. "All artists are influenced by other artists. Shakespeare comes to mind."

"And the more they use of someone else's work, the less they're making original art." He smiled. "I remember this argument, Mrs. J."

"Not argument. Discussion." She gave him a fond glance. "And you're wrong about yourself, you know. You're an artist. Always have been." She chuckled. "And don't you roll your eyes at me, young man."

"Sorry."

"I have an idea," Molly said. "I can see how welding during an art fair could be problematic. I didn't think that through. I also understand if you're not fond of being in the spotlight." She paused. "Would you consider doing it for an audience of one?"

Interesting idea. "You?" Sounded cozy. His libido grabbed the concept and ran with it. His cautious side waved a ginormous red flag.

"Me and a video camera. Grammy gave me one as an early Christmas present."

"You'd film me?" Ugh. No thanks. "I'm not crazy about someone taking a—"

"I'd be quiet. You'd forget I'm even there."

"Not a chance."

"Hear me out. Having someone you know take a short video has got to be less painful than performing for strangers. The video would give you presence in the booth. People might ask questions about it, and answering those would be better than standing around feeling uncomfortable."

"I do hate that." Her eager expression and coaxing tone were hard to resist. And when she looked at him with those big brown eyes, he'd say yes to almost anything. "We'd show the video in the booth?"

"Yes, possibly on a laptop, but ideally on a decent-sized computer monitor. I'm assuming the fair's indoors this time of year?"

"In the high school gym."

"Electrical hookups?"

"Yes, ma'am."

"Excellent. If you or Gil have a computer monitor you can set up in the booth, the video can run on a loop during the fair."

"That's doable."

"Then what do you say? People love seeing an artist at work. They like getting a glimpse into the process."

"It's worth a shot."

"Great! Do you have another fair scheduled soon?"

"This weekend. The annual Christmas fair. It'll be our first time there."

Grammy sighed. "I have great memories of that one. I went every year until... well, I haven't been in a while."

"Gil's ramped up about it." He turned to Molly. "But it's probably too soon for you to—"

"Not if we work fast. What's your current project?" Excitement gleamed in her eyes. "Is it something that would be relatable if I filmed it? Something connected to the holiday, maybe?"

"I have an order for twenty luminarias. I have to finish the last five tonight."

"That's perfect!" She practically bounced in her chair. "Do you have candles for the ones you've finished?"

"I don't. I was leaving that up to the customer."

"Grammy, do you—"

"I'm loaded with all sorts of candles. You should go over to his shop tonight and make that video."

"I was thinking the same thing, but would you be okay with postponing the tree decorating?"

"Of course. Tomorrow's better, anyway. We'll be fresh."

"Just to warn you, Molly, those luminarias will take at least two hours. I doubt you want to spend that much time on the video."

"I probably need that much time. I've never filmed anything like this before. I'll take a lot more footage than I'll use. Two hours sounds about right to me."

"Alrighty, then." And... he was in trouble. Making this video would mean they'd be alone in the shop. An extremely private situation. Not a whole lot could happen, because he'd be welding and she'd be filming.

But when they were done... well, that was the question, wasn't it? They'd both be tired, technically a plus. Except he was prone to bad decisions when he was tired.

He was so involved with that scenario that he almost missed the obvious glitch in the plan. "What if folks see the video and want to buy a luminaria? Other than the ones I'm making now, we don't have any in stock."

She blinked. "Good grief, you're right. I got carried away and didn't think of that important detail."

And he'd just poured cold water on her concept. "No reason you would, since you're not familiar with our operation. I should have thought of it sooner."

A frown had replaced her eager smile. "Then you don't take your products to the craft fairs?"

"A few small decorative items to hang on the wall, but not much. Gil put together a binder with pictures of what kinds of things we do. Projects are usually custom work. And we primarily work on commission."

She nodded. "Saves you making things you can't sell."

"Exactly. But this is our first year in business, our first Christmas season. The luminarias were a customer's idea, not mine. That said, I can see a potential market for them."

"I sure do. A festive item that will last from year to year, something that could be passed down — I think people will go for it. But if you don't have any in stock, then—"

"I could make some more between now and the fair."

"You could?" The light returned to her eyes.

"Not a ton, but at least so we'd have some. Gil's officially on vacation except for the fair this weekend, but he might see the benefit in this and pitch in."

"They could be a great ambassador for your business, especially if you tuck a business card inside. Unlike a wall hanging, a luminaria is something people use. They handle it. A small impulse buy could lead to a bigger purchase later."

"Or I could make a bunch and nobody wants them."

"Oh, they'll want them," Molly said. "I've seen how the live demonstrations push sales in the hotel lobby. The video will get the same response. Then if they catch on, you could make more at your leisure during the year so you're ready for next Christmas. I can see how this—"

"You need to quit talking and start doing." Mrs. J pushed back her chair and stood. "Go make this video."

"We'll help with the dishes, though." Bret left his chair and his boot connected with something under the table, sending it jingling and rolling along the hardwood floor. He knew a cat toy when he heard one. "Your cat must be shy, Mrs. J. I never guessed you had one."

"I don't have a—" She sucked in a breath and exchanged a quick glance with Molly. "Not *anymore*, that is. Not *now*."

"Oh." Damn. Must be dead, then. And recently if a toy was still lying around. "When did he or she… pass on?" He asked the question gently. His family grieved long and hard for every animal on the ranch.

Mrs. J and Molly spoke at once, with Mrs. J blurting out *a while ago* and Molly saying *last week.*

Molly flushed. "Time becomes so fluid when you've had a loss. Don't you agree, Bret?"

"Yes, ma'am." Something was fishy. These two weren't acting even slightly grief-stricken.

"Okay, I confess." Mrs. J ducked under the table and came up with the jingly ball. "I don't have a cat. I bought this at the Baby Barn because I love the way it sounds. I must have knocked it off the kitchen counter this afternoon and it rolled in here."

Huh? Bret stared at her, more confused than ever. Was she losing it?

"Let me explain. Tambourines were big in the sixties. Fooling with this reminds me of my short but memorable singing career." She tapped the ball against her palm a few times.

"You had a singing career?"

"Three friends and I. We were The Mellow Mushrooms. I gave away my tambourine years ago and kinda wish I hadn't."

"Why not just buy another one?"

She shrugged. "I'm not *that* into it. This works fine. I'll show you." Tapping the ball rhythmically against her palm, she swayed back and forth and sang the opening lyrics to *Mr. Tambourine Man.* Did a good job of it, too.

He couldn't have been more surprised if she'd sprouted wings and flown out the front door. Mrs. J was a champ at keeping order in the library and quick as silver in a debate. He'd never pegged her as a sixties flower child performing folk music with a group called the Mellow Mushrooms.

She paused. "You look a little dazed, dear boy."

"You took me by surprise, Mrs. J." He glanced at Molly, who'd ducked her head. He couldn't tell if she was embarrassed, laughing, or both.

"Everyone has hidden depths, you know."

"Clearly."

"Enough of this nonsense. It's late and you have a lot to do. I'll take care of the dishes."

"Thanks, Grammy." Cheeks pink and eyes sparkling, Molly came around the table and hugged her. Then she looked over at Bret. "Be right with you. I just need to get my camera bag." She left the room and hurried upstairs.

Bret turned to his hostess. "I'll at least help you clear the table."

"If you insist. I'll take the cake in if you'll gather up the dishes."

"Yes, ma'am." He stacked everything and carried it into the kitchen.

She lowered a glass cover over the cake. "You like her. I can tell."

"Of course I like her." He set the dishes and coffee cups on the counter. "She's terrific. But what are the chances she'll stay here? Jobs like hers are in the big city."

"For the most part. But don't get tangled up in the negatives. Keep an open mind."

"I'm just being realistic."

She frowned. "Evidently you've forgotten the sign I had at the library check-out desk."

"What sign?"

"Reality is for those who lack imagination."

"Ah. I do remember that one. Purple letters on a green background."

"That used to be your mantra."

"Sure. When you're seventeen, you believe anything's possible."

"I'm seventy-five, and I still believe anything's possible." She gazed at him. "I know you have an imagination, Bret. You use it in your work. When did you stop using it in your life?"

It was the kind of question a flower child of the sixties might ask. One with hidden depths. He didn't have a good answer.

4

Because it was snowing and predicted to continue, Molly agreed to ride over with Bret. Her little car wasn't great in the snow and she was more than happy to accept the added safety of his truck.

"Your grandmother cracks me up." He put her camera case and the box of votives in the back seat while she climbed in the front.

"She's something, all right." And resourceful. She must have forgotten to check under the table when she was picking up Zach's toys. He loved playing his baby version of pinball under there. He'd sit in the middle and smack the ball in hopes it would hit the chair or table legs and bounce back.

"I didn't know she was a singer."

"She loves it. My mom just had a couple of tapes digitized so we could hear The Mellow Mushrooms in action."

"I don't suppose you have them on your phone."

"Not yet. Mom's going to send me a copy, but life's been crazy and she hasn't gotten to it. I do have pictures she sent a couple of months ago.

Grammy had long hair, pink-tinged sunglasses, beads. You wouldn't recognize her."

He laughed. "Cue 'em up and you can show me before we take off." Closing the door, he hurried around the front of the truck. By the time he got behind the wheel, snow had gathered on the brim of his hat. He tapped it against the open door, laid it on the dash and pulled the door shut. "Coming down faster, now. Good thing you didn't take your little car."

"It's not so good in winter weather."

"That's okay. My truck is. Let me get the heater going." He turned the key and a Christmas carol drifted from the speakers.

She let out a happy sigh. "Nice."

"One of my favorite things about Christmas. The music."

"Me, too." She handed over her phone. "Here you go. There's only four. Wish we had more."

He looked at the first one and chuckled. "You're right. I'd never guess that was her." He swiped his finger across the screen until he'd seen all four, then went backwards. "All that hair. On the guys, too. Beards, headbands. They look happy, though."

"She says it was the most carefree time of her life. They traveled coast-to-coast, Boston to San Francisco. Grandpa Hank came to a performance in Missoula, gave her his phone number and made her promise to call him when she was done kicking up her heels. He'd wait for her."

"No kidding." He handed back the phone. "How long did he wait?"

"Two years. She called him, he sent her money for a bus ticket, and the rest is history."

"I guess he knew what he wanted when he saw it." Flipping on the wipers, he adjusted the air vents before he pulled away from the curb.

"So did Grammy. But she wasn't ready to settle down. When she finally called, she expected him to be married with kids. When he wasn't, she knew they were meant to be."

"That's quite a story."

"They got married a couple days before Christmas, so the holidays were always special for them."

"Must make it tough for her, now."

"It has been. But having me move in has helped her. It's helped me, too. Last year I couldn't find the Christmas spirit, no matter how hard I tried."

"That's to be expected, considering."

"I was afraid it might be gone for good. You know what? It's not. I've already had some Christmas spirit moments. I had one a little bit ago, when you turned the key and the music came on."

He smiled. "I'm glad. Music triggers it for me, too."

"It's such a special feeling, like a warm hug mixed with a zing of anticipation."

"For me it's like I'm a stack of pancakes that just got covered in warm maple syrup."

"That's a great description."

"Especially if you're into pancakes."

"Who isn't?" He was a sensual guy. She'd picked up on it during dinner. He'd savored every bite of food, especially the chocolate cake.

Some people ate mindlessly. Not Bret. Cooking for him, or better yet, cooking *with* him would be a pleasure. Enjoying the results together would be... her skin heated as her fantasy kicked into high gear.

He was the first dyed-in-the-wool cowboy she'd spent any time with and he fascinated her. Cocooned with him in the cab, she breathed in the leather scent of his jacket and the faint aroma of pine. Needles still clung to the creases in his sleeve.

He wore his thick brown hair cut short and his hat had left a furrow that she was tempted to reach over and smooth out. She didn't know him well enough, not yet.

She'd like to, but she'd already figured out they had a problem. He was firmly planted in Wagon Train and she'd have to go elsewhere to find a job. The only hotel in town, half the size of the one in Denver, was capably managed by the owner.

Getting involved with Bret made no sense, but doggone it, she liked him. For the first time in more than a year, she had the urge to touch and be touched by a man. He'd looked at her as if he'd like to do that, too.

His big hands rested loosely on the steering wheel, hands that could turn ordinary pieces of metal into works of art. That was sexy. But getting caught staring at him would be embarrassing. She glanced out the window and focused on the decorations as he turned onto Main Street.

"I'm curious about your small car."

"Oh?" Staring at him in the silent cab wasn't cool, but looking at him while they were talking was a whole other thing. Unless she lost her place in the conversation and went back to staring.

"Aren't winters intense in Boston? And Denver, for that matter."

"Yes, but both are tourist destinations in the summer and parking is nuts. In Boston I was the designated driver for my friends during the warm half of the year and I bummed a ride with them the other half."

"Ingenious. Did you work the same plan in Denver?"

"In a way." Her chest tightened the slightest bit. Not too bad, though. "Aaron had the SUV for the winter months and I had the good mileage car that fits in any parking space during the summer tourist season."

"I take it Aaron was your...."

"Husband. Yes." She quietly took a long, slow breath and let it out just as slowly. Better.

"We don't have to talk about him if you'd rather not."

"I'm okay talking about him, especially with people who don't start treating me like an invalid."

"I'd say you're more like a warrior. First you lose him and then you lose your job. I'm impressed that you kept going."

Because I have a son. But she couldn't tell him that. "Aaron's attitude helped. He had cancer and although his death was the worst nightmare I've ever lived through, it wasn't a surprise."

"Does that really help, though? Doesn't seem like it would."

"Sort of. We had time to… talk things out. He made me promise not to wallow, to look toward the future, to find—" *a new husband.* She swallowed. "Happiness."

"Sounds like a great guy."

"He was. The best. And keeping my promise to him has been good therapy." She let the sadness come and then gradually drift away. What had they been talking about? Oh, yeah. Her tiny car. "I'll bet you're wondering why I didn't keep his SUV and ditch my car."

"It crossed my mind."

She smiled. "That's what a man would do, I'll bet."

"I can't say for sure, but probably. Unless the engine leaked oil or there was a busted air conditioner."

"It was in top condition. I tried to keep it, but every time I got behind the wheel, I started crying."

"Mm."

The soft murmur of sympathy touched her. He got it. Her throat tightened.

Reaching over, he squeezed her shoulder. "Sorry."

"But then I realized that Aaron had wanted me to be happy. Driving his SUV didn't make me happy, so I sold it and used the money to get my car in better shape. I've had it since before I met him, so I could drive it without turning into a puddle. All that said, she still doesn't handle snow and ice very well."

"She?"

"Her name's Sally." She looked over in time to see his cheek dent in a smile. "Does that sound silly?"

"No. It sounds adorable."

"I realize I'm being impractical. But for the time being I have my bases covered. Grammy has a tough little Subaru that can handle this weather. She told me to take it tonight, but it's new and I was afraid pine needles and sap would get on the upholstery, even if I laid down a tarp. Needles are tricky little devils."

"You're telling me. I'll bet I have some in my underwear."

He'd likely meant it to be a joke, so she laughed, as if talking about his underwear didn't give her squiggles in her stomach. Nice squiggles. "Anyway, that tree wouldn't have fit in Grammy's Subaru, either."

"No, ma'am. You required a pickup. But that's probably the only time you'll need one, and your car will be perfect if you relocate to someplace warm, like Southern California."

"That's where my logic falls apart. I like living in snow country. Especially at Christmas."

"So do I." He drove slowly to the far end of Main Street, deserted at this hour. The steady cascade of flakes filled in tire tracks and settled in drifts along the sidewalk. "Snow makes everything look special this time of year. Palm trees and seventy degrees wouldn't work for me."

"I've never tried it and don't want to. Driving down this street with Christmas music and snow is the mood I'm looking for. I'm glad you had to go back. This is nice."

"I agree, but I'm worried that you'll get bored watching me weld for two hours straight."

"I promise I won't. You have no idea how eager I am to tackle this project."

"Maybe not."

"When I managed the El Capitan, every day brought a new creative challenge and I miss that. I need this project more than you need it done, so thank you." Much as she loved Zach, caring for him didn't use the full range of her abilities.

He chuckled. "Happy to help."

"I'm serious. Decorating the house with Grammy took the edge off, but now that's done. I spend a lot of time spinning my wheels."

"I understand that more than you can imagine. Gil was the one who suggested taking a bunch of time off over the holidays. I wondered what the heck I'd do with myself. I even thought of sneaking back to town and working in secret."

That made her grin. "You're no better at idleness than I am. We're the perfect pair to labor into the night."

"Guess so."

She gathered her courage. "Judging from what you said about sneaking in to work during your Christmas break, I'm thinking you don't have a special someone."

"Not at the moment." He dragged in a breath and let it out. "I'm probably about to make a fool of myself, but I feel like we need to get this out in the open."

"Grammy's matchmaking?"

"That's part of it." He made a left into the parking area in front of the shop. The tires crunched on fresh snow.

"Please forgive her. She desperately wants me to find a sweetheart and she gets a little heavy-handed at times, but—"

"I don't mind that. If circumstances were different, I'd be happy to fall right in with her plans." He kept the motor running. "I think you're amazing."

Her heartbeat picked up. "I think you're amazing, too."

Unbuckling his seat belt, he turned to her. "That's nice to hear. And if you were planning to establish a life for yourself in Wagon Train—"

"Which doesn't seem likely." In the faint light from the dash, his eyes were more gray than blue. Still mesmerizing, though. She took a breath. "You're looking for someone for the long haul."

"Yes, ma'am." His tone was low, sexy.

It sent shivers through her. "Me, too."

"Keeping your promise."

"Yes." Her gaze drifted to his lips. Chiseled. Tempting. "So the smart thing...."

"Would be to put a lid on this."

She couldn't resist asking, just to see what he'd say. "*This*?" She unfastened her seatbelt so she could face him.

"What's happening between us."

"So far that's nothing." Not quite true. Her body hummed with awareness. She had no business prolonging the exchange, but it was so delicious.

His eyes darkened. "So far."

Oh, man. Those eyes... "Do you want to kiss me, Bret?"

"Yes, ma'am."

She sucked in a breath.

His voice softened as he leaned closer. "And you want me to, Miss Molly."

"Uh-huh." *Do it.*

His attention settled on her mouth.

The pulsing of her heartbeat created a roaring in her ears. She closed her eyes.

"Been thinking about this ever since I met you."

His murmured words caused a slight breeze that gently brushed her lips. He was almost there....

And then he wasn't. With a groan of frustration, he backed off. When she opened her eyes, he was leaning his head against the frosty window.

His chest heaved. "That's what *this* is."

"I see." She struggled to get her breathing under control.

"And if I'd kissed you just now, we'd be steaming up the windows when I—"

"Need to work. My fault. It's been so long since I've been in this situation."

"I've never been in this situation. I don't normally visualize kissing a woman minutes after laying eyes on her."

"And I don't normally meet a man and shortly thereafter ogle his butt."

He grinned. "You did?"

"Afraid so."

"Seems like we're both in uncharted territory."

"True, but you have work to do and I had no business asking about your social life."

"It's not like I haven't been thinking about you. And trying to figure out if there's any way. But we're moving in different directions." Reaching behind him, he opened his door. "I'll leave the motor running. It'll be better if you stay here for a sec while I get the door open, secure Rivet and turn on some lights."

"Who's Rivet?"

"Our office cat. See you in a few." And he was gone, swallowed by the snowy night.

Well, dammit. After worrying that her urge to merge had disappeared, she'd found a man who inspired all the feels. And he was the wrong man.

5

The minute Bret slipped inside and shut the door behind him, Rivet came running, her tail in the air and rapid little meows of welcome filling the silence.

He crouched briefly to stroke her arched back. "Hey, Rivet. I have someone waiting in the truck, so I need to go bring her in. Her name's Molly and she's nice, but don't get attached, okay?"

The calico responded with a deep purr that vibrated her whole body.

"I mean it. She'll be gone before you know it." Rising quickly to his feet, he headed for the back room, Rivet close on his heels. She'd been asleep when he'd left for the tree lot which meant she'd missed dinner. "I promise to feed you as soon as I get Molly and her stuff inside."

After hitting the light switch, he grabbed the old army blanket from the daybed against the right-hand wall. He and Gil had created a micro-apartment back there.

Couldn't even qualify as an efficiency, but if either of them wanted to stay in town overnight, it sufficed. On nights before a craft fair, they both stayed here and flipped a coin to see who got the bed and who had to make do with a sleeping bag on the floor.

The bed was the only piece of furniture. The bathroom was compact but functional and had a small shower. A fridge, stove, sink and short counter with drawers underneath and a cabinet above made up the bare-bones kitchen.

Giving Rivet orders to stay put, he left the shop holding the blanket over his head. Luckily he didn't have to deal with wind as he plowed through the snow to the truck.

Uh-oh. Spoke too soon. The wind whipped up right as he reached the passenger door. He opened it a crack. "I'll get you inside and come back for the camera bag and candles."

"I can carry—"

"Wind's getting nasty and the footing isn't great. Come with me, please."

"You bet."

"Thanks." As he held the blanket up to shield her from the worst of the snow, she hopped down and closed the door behind her.

"Brrr. You weren't kidding."

"No, ma'am. Follow the trail I made. I'll be right behind you. Too bad you didn't wear boots, but no point in worrying about it, now."

"My shoes will dry." She started off and he lifted the blanket over her head.

"If not, we can use my torch on 'em."

"I think not."

"Don't worry. I'm a master of the slow burn."

She laughed. "I'll bet you say that to all the girls."

"Nope. You're the first one I've tried it on. What do you think?"

"A little too on the nose."

"Story of my life. Just go straight in. Don't hesitate. Rivet's normally too smart to try and get out in this weather, but I don't want to take any chances."

"Got it." Molly moved fast and they made it through the door without incident.

Turned out Rivet had stayed put, after all. She approached cautiously, her tail still up but her steps slow and deliberate. Her attention was glued to the stranger.

"Rivet, this is Molly. Molly, meet Rivet, our weird shop cat. She loves the smell of hot metal. I close her in back when I'm working, and the minute I let her out, she heads for the welding table to get her fix."

Molly crouched down and held out her hand, palm down. "Hey, Rivet. We all have our peculiar preferences. I love the smell of gasoline."

That tickled him. "Raised in a filling station, were you?"

"No, but we took lots of cross-country road trips when I was a kid. I was allowed to help fill the tank. Gas smells like adventure, adventure with people you love."

"Nicely put."

Rivet took her time sniffing the newcomer's hand. Molly stayed motionless, making no attempt to pet the cat. Instead she continued talking to her, encouraging her to indulge in whatever smell she most enjoyed.

"You've been around kitties."

"We had a tux when I was growing up. Aaron was allergic, so we didn't have a cat, but… oh, Rivet, did I pass the test?"

Rivet nudged her hand, a clear invitation to deepen the relationship. Molly obliged with chin rubs and ear scratches.

"You definitely passed the test. She'll love you forever." His advice to Rivet had fallen on deaf ears. In no time at all, that kitty had become attached. She'd have to learn the hard way when Molly left town. "While you two get better acquainted, I'll fetch your camera bag and the candles."

She glanced up. "If you're not back in ten minutes I'll send Rivet with a keg of brandy around her neck."

That made him smile. "Thanks." She would have to dish his brand of humor. He was in danger of making the same mistake as his cat, letting down his guard, allowing himself to get attached.

But damn it, how was he supposed to keep up his defenses with a woman who'd made friends with his cat and cracked good jokes? Kissable mouth and tempting body aside, she was also fun. *What's your plan, now, genius?*

He grabbed the blanket to protect the box of candles and headed for the door. When he opened it, snow smacked him in the face and nearly took off his hat. Clamping it to his head, he charged outside as Molly called out a quick *be careful* before she slammed the door shut.

Too late for that warning. The storm wasn't his biggest problem, but it could add to his dilemma about Molly if they got snowed in. Hadn't considered that tiny detail, had he?

At least he'd been smart enough to bring the blanket. Draping it over his head, he grabbed it under his chin to anchor the hat, dropped his shoulder linebacker style and forced his way through the gusts. He tried to hold the blanket closed with his other hand, but finally gave up and let it billow around him. A caped crusader. Ha.

The truck's back door latch was frozen. Digging in his heels, he yanked hard. The door popped open and wind blew snow into the back seat. He blocked the opening with his body while he slung the camera case strap over his left shoulder, which pinned the blanket in place on that side. He stuffed the box of candles inside his jacket.

After an epic struggle with Mother Nature, he managed to close the door. At least on the return trip the wind would be at his back. But it had risen to gale force and damn near blew him over.

He dug in his heels. Smooth leather soles were great for dancing at the Fluffy Buffalo. Not so good for plowing through this junk. He had a pair of snow boots in the back of the shop, but had he remembered that? Nope. He'd had Molly on the brain.

Managing the doorknob would be tricky when he needed both hands to keep the blanket secured and the candles inside his jacket. Maybe if he—

The door opened. “Get in here!”

He dashed through the opening and turned. She’d probably need help with—nope, she was on it.

Shoulder to the door, she gave a mighty shove, rammed it shut and flipped the security latch. Then she faced him, her expression triumphant. “Told you I’m stronger than I look.”

He grinned. Yep, he really liked her. “Well done.” Handing her the camera case and the candles, he took off the wet blanket and his slightly less soaked hat. “I’ll go drape this over the shower stall door.” Rivet followed him as he carried the blanket and his hat through the shop.

“You have quite a homey setup back there.”

So she’d taken a peek. “It’s handy,” he called over his shoulder. “Speaking of homey, want something warm to drink?”

“Sounds nice.”

He raised his voice. “Like what?” Folding the blanket in thirds, he tucked it over the glass door of the bathroom’s shower stall. Not a perfect drying rack, but it would do.

“Whatcha got?”

He came out and found her standing just inside the doorway. The wind continued to howl, rattling the panes in the small window over the bed, emphasizing the cozy nature of this moment. If he looked into her eyes, he’d be a goner.

He glanced at the coffeepot on the counter. "I can make coffee, or I can warm up some cider."

She moved fully into the space, her breathing a little fast. "Coffee, please. Warm cider will put me to sleep."

Sure it would. Not when her voice had that little quiver. She was keyed up, too. "Coffee it is." He started to peel off his jacket and paused. "Did you hang your coat up front?"

"I did. There must be fifty or sixty horseshoes in that coat rack. Impressive engineering."

"Thank you. It was a challenge. But your coat will dry better on a hanger back here." He gestured toward a small nook where they'd mounted a rod that could hold a change of clothes and the inevitable wet jacket. "That's what I'm doing with mine."

"Sounds like a plan." She headed to the front of the shop.

"I'll start the coffee."

Rivet let out a pitiful meow.

"Right after I feed you, of course." He picked up her dish to clean it and Rivet promptly sat in front of her food mat, waiting to be served. He was drying the dish when Molly reappeared. "Coffee's not started yet. I promised to feed—"

"I'd be happy to do it." Molly hung up her coat with brisk efficiency and came over to the sink. "Where's her food?"

"In a Tupperware jar in the fridge. Her name's on the lid."

"So you won't accidentally eat the cat's food?"

He chuckled. "Something like that." After handing over the bowl, he pulled a tablespoon from a large ceramic jug stuffed with silverware and cooking utensils. "Two spoonfuls. And thanks."

"It's fun for me. Rivet reminds me how much I enjoyed having a cat."

While he ground the coffee beans, Molly dished out Rivet's food with brisk efficiency. She talked to the cat the whole time and Rivet talked back. She'd accepted Molly as a member of the family.

He pulled mugs out of the cupboard over the sink. "Cream? Sugar?"

"Neither, thanks."

"Simplifies things."

"I try to do that whenever I can. Life's complicated enough as it is."

Especially with the setbacks you've had. Her resiliency added another layer to his respect for the lady. And then there was the chemistry. Couldn't seem to ignore that sensual urge.

But surrendering to it was asking for trouble. Talk about complications. He needed to douse that fire licking at his privates.

Easier said than done.

6

Stranded with a hot cowboy in a snowstorm. Classic. Working side-by-side with Bret in the tiny kitchen space, Molly welcomed her first genuine case of lust since her world had fallen apart.

Maybe, just maybe, she could put it back together. Probably not with this guy. But her full-throttle reaction to him gave her hope. She had a shot at fulfilling her promise to Aaron.

Too bad Bret couldn't be the one to help her with that. His manly presence warmed her all the way down to her ankles. She couldn't include her toes in that assessment, though. Her wet loafers and clammy socks had given her cold feet. Ha, ha.

Just as well. Getting chummy would be a mistake in the long run and in the short run. They had things to accomplish.

She believed in this video and wanted to make it work. A video could boost sales at fairs, but it could also harness the power of the internet. Had McLintock Metalworks made full use of that?

"Coffee's almost done."

"So's Rivet's dinner."

"Yeah, it's a little later than usual, so she's probably famished. Sorry, Rivet."

The calico paused to glance over her shoulder at him. Then she went back to eating.

Molly flashed him a grin. "Did you see that look?"

"Yes, ma'am. She loves making me feel guilty."

"That's obvious. Hey, total change in subject, do you and Gil have a YouTube channel?"

"A what?"

"That answers my question. I'd advise looking into it, assuming the video turns out to be something you're proud of. If you get an account, you could consider making instructional videos. That can generate business."

He leaned his hips against the kitchen counter and crossed his arms. "I have a vague concept of what you're talking about, but I'm not a born teacher. I've seen folks who can talk and work. Gil might be able to do it, but I'm not your guy."

Also true on a personal level, darn it. "I'm just throwing stuff out there." *Better than throwing myself at you.* "Because El Capitan was a family-owned hotel with a relatively small budget, we didn't have a professional marketer. I was it. I learned on the job."

"But that was a hotel and this is—"

"No different. Not really. But if you're happy with the status-quo—"

"We're a startup. We can't afford to be happy with the status quo. I'll mention the Youtube channel to Gil. I can see him making a how-to video. He'd be good at it."

"Since I'm new in town, I haven't met him yet. Does he look like you?" If he was drop-dead handsome like Bret, that would boost views.

"Kind of. His hair has a reddish tinge, like my mom's, and his eyes are very blue, like our dad's, whereas mine are a mix of blue and green."

"I noticed. It depends on the light which they are."

"Or what I'm wearing."

"You and Gil have the same dad?" Grammy seemed to think every kid had a different father and she was clearly fascinated by that. Her comment that *Desiree McLintock makes her own rules* had been filled with admiration for the town's most prominent citizen.

He smiled. "Mrs. J must have given you some of our history."

"Like I said, she thinks a lot of your family. But she was under the impression no two kids had the same dad."

"Gil and I are the only ones. They broke up after I was born. Then they made up again long enough to conceive Gil. They just— well, it's a long story."

"I'll bet it's an interesting one." Her cold toes began to cramp. She shifted her weight, doing her best to be subtle. "You might not have time to tell me tonight, but at some point—"

"Hang on." His gaze sharpened. Then he broke eye contact and looked down at her feet. "I'm an idiot. Your shoes are soaked. You need to get 'em off."

"I'm okay." Walking around barefoot wouldn't be any better.

"I have a pair of heavy socks you can borrow. How about putting those on?"

Ahhh. He could do something about it. "Yes, please."

"I should have thought of it sooner." He crossed to the rudimentary closet, reached up to a shelf mounted above the rod and took down a pair of thick gray socks.

His, most likely. He wasn't going to loan out Gil's. "Here you go."

"Thanks!" She sat on the bed because that was the only available surface. "Did somebody knit these?"

"Colleen. She's one of the Wenches. Do you know—"

"Your mom's book club. Grammy told me all about that."

"Colleen started out crocheting, and then she got into knitting. She gave me these back in October. All the kids have a pair."

"Just one pair?" She clutched the socks, longing to put them on but worried they were too precious to wear.

"Just one pair each, but I've worn them constantly and they wash up great, so don't treat them like an heirloom."

"Exactly what I was thinking I should do."

"Colleen told us to wear them, not tuck them away for fear they'd get ruined. Since we all like them so much, she's making more."

"You're lucky that she's doing that. The yarn is incredible." Molly held it up to her cheek. "I think this is what they mean with the phrase *soft as a baby's bottom.*"

"I can't say, since it's been a long time since I've touched a baby's bottom."

Not her. More like a few hours ago. "Doesn't matter. Just one of those expressions everybody says." Pulling off her loafers and clammy socks with a sigh of relief, she picked up the first sock.

"Wait. Let me get you a towel to dry off."

She glanced up and met the sweetest expression of concern in those green-blue eyes. Grammy had it right. Bret was a special guy. "Thanks."

He ducked into the bathroom, came out with a bath towel and handed it to her. "One advantage of this small space. Everything's within reach."

Including you. The combination of a hard body and a soft heart was tough to resist. But the man had work to do. She concentrated on her feet. "How's the coffee coming along?" She used her back-to-business voice.

"It's done."

"Let's take it out to the shop. You can show me around before you get back to your welding."

"Good idea."

He'd adopted the same tone. Mission accomplished. Moments later they strolled, coffee mugs in hand, through the shop.

Her toes were in heaven. Sadly, that allowed the rest of her to fully respond to the tempting sexuality of her guide as he pointed out the tools of his trade.

She admired the completed luminarias, sections of steel pipe with a welded bottom and intricate cutouts to let candlelight through. She'd expected them to look good, but the precision and artistry in the stars, snowflakes, holly and bells went way beyond her expectations. "Stunning, Bret."

"Thank you." He flushed slightly.

"You do welding *and* blacksmithing to create things?"

"Yes, ma'am. When Gil and I decided to move into metal art, some folks advised us to switch to welding for that and save the forge and anvil for shoeing horses. But I like using my blacksmithing to do creative things, too."

"I see the anvil, but where's the forge? Isn't that like a fire pit?"

"Not if it's gas." He pointed to a boxy contraption on a stand. "That's way safer and cleaner. A coal fire is smoky and dirty. I have a coal forge at home, though. Still love working with it. But that's not practical in here."

"Makes sense. Why is there so much more stuff on the blacksmith side? The welding side looks almost like an operating room."

"That's on purpose. Can't have anything flammable in the area. We've fireproofed the walls, the tables and the floor."

"How close can I get when I film?"

"No more than fifteen feet."

"Good thing I have a zoom. Ready to start?"

He consulted an old-fashioned wall clock hung on the blacksmith side. "Probably should. Don't want to keep you too late." He polished off his coffee and set the mug next to the cash register. "Are you gonna alert me when you start filming?"

"Do you want me to?"

"Might be better if you don't. I'll try to forget you're there, like you said earlier. Just promise me you'll stay back."

"I promise."

He looked down at her feet. "Wearing those socks will make you silent as a cat, so I probably won't hear you. Which reminds me, I need to close Rivet in the back."

"Where is she?" Molly glanced around the shop. No cat.

"Probably on the bed taking her after-dinner snooze. I'll go close the door."

As he headed toward the back, she finished her coffee, picked up her camera case and set it on the counter.

"Molly?"

She looked up.

He stood near the door. "I didn't react so well when you first suggested taking this video."

"No worries. Lots of people are camera shy."

"But it was a kind offer meant to help me. Help the business. I'm grateful and I don't remember saying so."

What a lovely speech. What a gorgeous man. She could stare into those blue-green eyes for hours. Staying businesslike wasn't easy, but she gave it a shot. "I'm not sure if you thanked me or not, but I consider us even. You're doing me a favor by giving me something interesting to do."

"You say that, but I have a hunch watching me weld these luminarias will be about as exciting as watching paint dry."

"I have a hunch I'll be fascinated."

"If you say so." He peeked in the back room and quietly closed the door.

Oh, she'd be fascinated, all right. Filming him using a fiery torch was liable to get her hotter than the metal he stroked with that sexy tongue of flame.

7

Bret hated being watched while he worked. Molly taking a video would be ten times worse. But her earnest request and the soft glow in her beautiful brown eyes had landed him in this pickle. Had to go through with it.

Doing his best to ignore her, he put on his protective apron, goggles and gauntlet-styled gloves. Then he adjusted the torch valves and lit it up. Although he didn't look in her direction, he could hear her breathing. Yeah, this would be torture.

He'd never been so wrong. Two minutes into the session, he was riding a creative high that left him breathless. Fully aware that her camera lens recorded his every move, he was all in, pushing himself to new levels of excellence.

He didn't care what the world thought of his technique, but he cared what Molly thought. He was — so embarrassing to admit it — showing off.

He never did that. He scoffed at guys who drove too fast, pinstriped their pickups, bought tight shirts to emphasize their pecs, stuffed socks in their jeans so they'd look generously endowed.

Just because he'd never use those cheesy methods didn't mean he wasn't engaged in the same game. She'd raved about his skill in creating the designs on the finished pieces. He was out to show her the full range of his abilities. Strutting like a rooster. He laughed at himself, but he didn't stop doing it.

He'd been pleased with the first fifteen. But number sixteen, the first one he created under the watchful eye of Molly's lens, was effing brilliant.

Praising his own work wasn't part of his routine, either. At least not until now, when Molly would be the first person to see the finished product and he was pulling out all the stops to impress the hell out of her.

And why? Getting involved with her made no sense. Laboring this hard to make her eyes light up and her breath catch was a crazy waste of energy.

Didn't matter. He kept pursuing that course of action, putting even more effort into the next one. Like it or not, he'd stumbled into the courtship dance.

Since he'd precut the lengths of pipe, he could finish one luminaria and move right on to the next. During the transition he caught a brief glimpse of Molly. She gave him a quick thumbs-up.

He gave her a jaunty grin. Because that's how the cool guy wielding a bad-ass torch would respond. If Gil could see him, he'd laugh his head off.

Between the second and third luminaria, he looked up to give his out-of-control ego another boost. She wasn't filming him anymore. Instead she'd set her camera down so she could put candles in the ones he'd finished.

She turned toward him. "Matches?"

"Want to use my torch?" Oh, yeah, he was hilarious.

"Ha, ha."

He reined in his runaway bravado. "There's an old box of matches in the back, in the drawer beside the sink." He positioned the section of pipe on the metal table. "Be stealthy. Don't let Rivet out."

"You know what? I'd rather not take the chance that she might get past me. I'll play around with filming through the window to see if I can capture the falling snow."

"Okay." Probably better if she didn't try to fetch the matches. Rivet was an escape artist.

The adrenaline rush of absorbing her total focus faded while she experimented with capturing the snow through the window. Just as well. He was in danger of getting hooked on it. And on Molly.

The previously charged atmosphere softened to cozy companionship — Molly doing her job while he did his. Nice. He liked working at night. Cut down on interruptions. But sometimes it was lonely.

The more time he spent with Molly, the better he appreciated her. She deserved a tangible reward, and he had the perfect thing.

Tomorrow, when he started making a batch of luminarias for the fair, first he'd make one for her. No, he'd make two. That way she could pair them up, maybe put one on either side of the porch steps.

Yeah, like that urge wasn't a signal that he wanted to take this beyond a casual friendship. He'd just dreamed up a way to give her a Christmas present. Maybe he should say it was for her and Mrs. J.

Except it wouldn't be. He appreciated Mrs. J a whole lot. But he'd be making his handcrafted Christmas gift so he could see the sparkle in Molly's dark eyes when she opened it. And hear her little gasp of delight.

He moved on to the fourth luminaria. His muscles protested the length of time in one position. He shifted his weight on the stool and took a deep breath. At least he'd streamlined the process along the way, so these last few had gone faster than the first batch.

Add in the adrenaline rush of Molly's presence and he'd increased his productivity by a lot. A quick glance at the wall clock confirmed that he'd finish in under two hours. Ignoring the sweat trickling down the side of his face, he picked up the fifth section of pipe.

"That's the last one, right?"

Her voice startled him. He moved the torch away from the pipe and located her standing a distance away, her camera lifted, ready to film. "Last one." His voice cracked. The water bottle he'd used this afternoon sat over on Gil's table, half-full but out of reach. He must have shifted it over there at some point so he had more room to work.

"You have to be exhausted."

"No, ma'am." He should be. His muscles ached and his throat was drier than boot leather, but he was wide awake. "Were you able to get the snowflakes to show up in the video?"

"Not really. I found a how-to online, though. It's trickier than I thought, and I need some supplies to pull it off."

"I'm sure it'll be great without that."

"I'm not giving up. I have two days to fiddle around. That's assuming you don't mind me trying again with tomorrow's batch and we get a little more snow."

An ongoing project that would bring her over here tomorrow. He liked the sound of that. "I can supply the luminarias. Can't guarantee falling snow."

"Sure you can. Just climb up on the roof and brush a little over the edge." She giggled. "I'm kidding. You should see your face. You're all *what the hell?*"

"On second thought, it might work."

"But we'll never know because you could fall and break your neck. Anyway, I didn't mean to slow you down." She made a shooing motion with her free hand. "Please continue. I'll film you making this last one. Getting some footage when you're sweaty will add authenticity."

"In other words, I'm a hot mess."

"Looks good on you." Her eyes gleamed the way they had when he'd almost kissed her.

He sucked in a quick breath. "I'll get to it, then." He laid the section of pipe on the table and made the first cut.

Although he couldn't see what she was doing with that camera, guaranteed she was trying to make him look sexy. And he was playing to it.

Meanwhile her undivided attention worked on him like an aphrodisiac. His sore muscles weren't the only part starting to ache.

He completed the piece as if moving toward a climax. Welding hadn't had sexual overtones this afternoon. It did tonight. When he was finished, he stepped back, flame still arcing from his torch. "Done."

"Beautiful." The word came out on a sigh.

"Thank you." He met her gaze. Oh, yeah, she wanted to be kissed. Thoroughly.

Breaking eye contact, he turned off the flame. "There's a procedure to shutting down that takes a few minutes, but it's safe for you to fetch the matches and let Rivet out."

"Okay, I'll do that." Her voice had a low, throaty quality.

His body responded, but he forced himself to concentrate on the sequence of switching off valves. Carelessness at this stage could cause major problems.

Rivet trotted out, her rapid-fire meows letting him know she didn't appreciate being confined. She headed straight for him.

"Rivet, *sit*." He looked her in the eye and presented his no-nonsense face.

Her haunches dropped immediately.

It was the only command she deigned to obey and he saved it for when he had hot metal on the table and didn't want her up there. "Good kitty."

She gave him a haughty stare.

"Sorry, that was patronizing. Thank you for your cooperation."

She began washing her face, as if sitting there had been her plan all along. Heaven forbid he should think he was the boss of her.

Grabbing a pair of tongs, he transferred the luminarias to a cooling shelf hanging seven feet above the floor and six feet from the edge of the table. Even a champion jumper like Rivet couldn't make that leap. Not that she hadn't tried.

He laid the tongs on the table and looked at her. "Okay, you can get up." He moved over to Gil's table, picked up his water bottle and took several long swallows while keeping an eye on Rivet.

She rose slowly and arched her back. Then she crouched, leaped to the table and sniffed where the hot metal had been. Her loud purr sounded like an electric razor. Crazy cat.

But what had happened to Molly? She should be back with the matches by now. "Hey, Molly, are you having trouble finding the—"

"Found 'em!" Her voice sounded funny, like something had happened during the search.

"Everything okay?"

"Absolutely! They just weren't in the top drawer like you said."

"Oh?" He started back there. "Where were they?"

"Bottom drawer."

"That's Gil's drawer. He must have moved them." Whoops. His brother kept something else in that drawer. No wonder Molly was acting discombobulated.

She came through the door, an old box of kitchen matches in her hand and roses in her cheeks. "Are you saying those aren't yours?"

"Not mine. Gil seemed to think he might... I mean depending on how things went during a night of dancing at the Buffalo... but so far he's never..." *Shut up, doofus.*

"I noticed the box hasn't been opened."

So she'd checked. Maybe to see if he brought women here on a regular basis. "I forgot they were there."

"Then you don't have any tucked away, just in case?"

He shook his head. "Taking a woman out dancing and then bringing her here wouldn't be my style. I question whether it's Gil's style, but after we rented this space and put in the amenities, he pictured that scenario." And talking about it was having a predictable effect. He glanced away, wrestled with his conscience.

"If you're embarrassed, please don't be. I'm not."

He made the mistake of looking into her velvet brown eyes. What he saw there sent heat spiraling through him. It settled in his groin. "I'm not embarrassed."

"Turned on, maybe?" She stepped closer.

"Yes, ma'am." He breathed deep. Her scent made him forget why he shouldn't kiss her. "That would be it." Her lips were so plump and tempting. Then she ran her tongue over them.

He threw in the towel, hauled her into his arms and claimed that luscious mouth. The taste of her wrenched a groan from his chest. He was done for.

She kissed him back with an enthusiasm that set him on fire. Dropping the matches, she grabbed onto him with both hands. The ancient box slid open on the way down and matches scattered everywhere.

They crunched under his boots as he swept her up in his arms and carried her through the doorway. Laying her on the bed, he lifted his head and gulped for air. "I swore I wasn't going to do this." He stood, losing himself in her hot gaze.

She drew in a quick breath. "You'd better not be changing your mind."

"No, ma'am." He turned, took three strides and wrenched open the bottom drawer. "I'm just fetching supplies. And closing the door."

8

Molly had lost her mind. Gloriously, completely lost it. And she didn't care. She let Bret, a man she'd met only hours ago, take off her clothes. And the socks he'd loaned her. She even helped him with the zipper on her jeans and then wiggled out of them with shocking eagerness.

When he started stripping off his clothes, she gave him her complete attention. She ran short of air as he revealed the muscular body she'd envisioned while he hunched over his work, conjuring up magic with fire and steel.

Thank goodness he didn't waste any time. In less than a minute he stood before her in all his manly glory.

And oh, how she wanted him. Craved him with an intensity that made her thighs slick and her nipples ache.

When he looked at her with those blue-green eyes, when his gaze traveled hungrily over her body, the sudden clench in her core made her gasp. She held out her hand. "Now. Please."

"Yes, ma'am." He made short work of the shrink-wrapped box, ripped open the packet and rolled on a condom. "We don't have much room."

"We have enough." Trembling with excitement, she beckoned him down. "We can make it work."

The corners of his mouth lifted. "Is this a project?"

"Yes! It's Project Molly!"

Laughter rumbled in his chest.

"Oh, wait, that sounds selfish. I want you to have a good time, too."

"I plan to, Miss Molly. I plan to." He lowered himself carefully to the bed and moved between her open thighs. "I'm going for a good time all around." He braced himself above her.

Reaching up, she cupped his face and her palms encountered the prickle of his beard. She didn't have much breath available. "Let me... say something."

His eyes glittered. "Make it quick."

"This... this doesn't mean we...." She trailed off as words failed her.

"No worries, Molly-girl." He paused, his voice husky. "It just means we like each other."

She swallowed. "Perfect."

"I do like you, Molly." He eased forward.

She clutched his shoulders and held his gaze. "I can't believe... how much I want you... inside me."

"I want to be there." He sank deeper.

The intense friction spiraled out, spreading pleasure to her breasts, her thighs, her fingers, her toes. The first spasm caught her by surprise. She gasped.

His eyes widened. "Molly?"

"I..." She gasped again and gripped his shoulders. "I'm..."

"Yes, you sure are. Let me help." He began to stroke.

And she was there, spinning out of control, crying out as waves of pleasure carried her to a place of joyful release, a familiar place. Yet different, more intense, more... primal.

His steady thrusts intensified the sensations coursing through her body. When she arched upward, he slipped his arm under the small of her back, holding her steady as he continued to move.

Gradually the undulations slowed, and he eased up on the pace until the moment he went completely still. Looking into her eyes, he smiled. "Was that what you had in mind?"

"Mostly, except..."

"Except?"

"It's a lot more fun if you come, too."

He nudged his way in a little deeper. "I'm not going anywhere. When you're ready, we'll try it again."

She stroked his broad shoulders and looked into his amazing eyes. "You're good at this, aren't you?"

"Next question, please."

"You don't have to tell me. I know you are." She met his gaze. "Why does your brother have condoms stashed back here and you don't?"

"Because this bed's too small for having decent sex, and I—"

"How about indecent sex?"

"No such thing." He lowered his head and brushed his lips over hers. "But I wouldn't have chosen this bed, this place, if I'd known...."

"How could you know?" She caressed his sweat-slicked back. "I didn't know. We just met. I've never in my life—"

"Same here, Miss Molly." He nibbled on her bottom lip and lowered his chest until the soft hair lightly touched her nipples. "I like working up to this."

"Then what happened?"

"I haven't figured that out, yet." He dropped light kisses on her cheeks as he began moving his hips in slow, easy strokes. "I just know when you gave me the green light, I couldn't hold back."

"I didn't want you to." Wrapping her arms around his warm, solid torso, she held on as he established a lazy rhythm. "I've been thinking about this ever since...." She hesitated. Maybe she shouldn't say *that.*

"Ever since what?"

"I don't want you thinking I'm obsessed with... male equipment."

"Why not? Most men, including me, are obsessed with female equipment." He continued to rock slowly back and forth.

And she, much to her surprise, was going to come again. Not immediately, but soon. Yes, he was very good at this.

He nipped playfully at her nose. "C'mon, Molly-girl. Tell me when you first started imagining us getting horizontal."

"When we put up the tree. I was under there tightening bolts."

"I'm aware." He held her gaze as he increased the pace, just a little.

"When I looked up through the branches, your zipper and...what was behind it...were perfectly framed by evergreen sprigs." Currently, that part of his anatomy was slowly but surely turning her inside out. Again.

"Planned that well, didn't I?"

"You meant for me to look?"

He chuckled. "No, but I'm glad you did. Meanwhile your cute little ass was sticking up giving me ideas."

"Really?"

"Yes, ma'am. The minute you crawled under that tree, I could imagine—" He slid his hand under her bottom and squeezed. "I just knew you'd feel good. I was right." He tightened his grip and lifted her slightly, enough to change the angle.

"*Oh.*" She gulped as each thrust touched off a surge of added pleasure. "That's...that's...nice."

"I think I've found the lady's G-spot."

"I...don't..." Words failed her. She could only moan as he picked up speed, pushing her toward the brink. Her moans became whimpers, then cries, then a lusty shout of triumph when he sent her hurtling over the edge.

Falling, swirling, surrendering to the buffeting winds of a powerful climax, she clung to him as he continued to stroke, prolonging the bliss. At last, with a sharp gasp, he drove in deep and stayed, leaning his forehead against her shoulder, his ragged breathing warming her skin as he shuddered in the grip of his release.

She held him tight, absorbing the shock waves, reveling in his low groan of satisfaction. So this was what sex could be like. Who knew?

9

Of course, the sex had to be spectacular. Of course it did. Bret wasn't one to avoid issues, so when he could speak without gasping, he lifted his head and gazed down at Molly. Beautiful Molly. "That went pretty well."

She smiled, a post-orgasmic softness in her eyes, an appealing flush on her cheeks. "Understatement."

He smiled back. Just the kind of remark he'd expect from her. "Awesome?"

"Epic."

"That, too. And it leaves us with some things to discuss."

"I know."

"Do you want to talk in bed and naked or out of bed and dressed?"

"In bed and naked."

"Then I'll be back in a few minutes." Easing away from her in the cramped space was a challenge, but he managed. "If you get cold, go ahead and slide under the covers."

"Okay."

He stepped into the bathroom and dealt with the condom. Gil would have a field day with this. Unless the open box disappeared and an unopened one took its place.

When he returned to the bed, Molly lay on her side under the covers.

Scooting up against the wall, she lifted the covers. "Come on in. I made as much room as I could."

"Thanks." He levered himself into the narrow space, bringing his body into contact with hers at several significant points.

"Is your brother as big as you?"

"He's half-an-inch shorter, which he doesn't like to talk about."

She grinned. "But you love talking about it, don't you?"

"Yes, ma'am. Every chance I get."

"I'm surprised he didn't lobby for a double, since he planned on getting jiggy here."

"He did, but it wouldn't fit between the door and the wall."

Lifting her head, she peered at the closed door. "I see what you mean." Then she glanced at him. "This'll work better if we slide our arms under each other's neck."

"Good idea. Any suggestions for where to put my other arm?"

"Whatever appeals to you."

"That's easy." Laughing, he cupped her ass.

"Two can play that game." She grabbed onto his.

He lay still, gazing into her eyes. "I want to kiss you."

"You start doing that and we won't get much talking done."

"We probably should have put on our clothes."

"I didn't want to."

"Me, either, but... will your grandmother wait up?"

"Heavens, no." Every time she took a breath, her nipples brushed his chest. "I guess you didn't hear her tell me not to rush back."

"I missed that. I don't want her to be worried about you."

"I guarantee she won't worry. I'm with you."

His conscience pricked him. "I doubt she'd approve of—"

"You might be surprised."

"Oh, I know she likes me and would like to see us get chummy, but not this fast." Or this often. He wanted her again. "Are you planning to tell her?"

"I might not have a choice. I think she'll pick up on it."

He sighed. "So will Gil. I considered switching out the condom box for a new one, but chances are he'd still—"

"Looks like there's no point in trying to keep it a secret." Her breathing had changed and her grip on his ass had turned into a slow massage.

And he was as hard as the steel he'd worked on tonight. "Then we'll go public."

"I think we have to, unless..." She dragged in air, her tight nipples caressing him, driving him closer to the point of no return.

"Unless?" He couldn't hold out much longer.

"We decide not to do this again."

"You mean *now*? Because—"

"Oh, we're doing this again tonight, buster."

"Thank you." He pulled her close, pressing his aching cock against her warm skin. "I—"

"I mean after that."

"Let's decide later."

"But—"

"Later." He covered her mouth with his, delving deep, swallowing her moan of surrender, kissing her until they both ran out of air.

Then he moved lower and captured her nipple between his teeth, biting gently before drawing her in. Her soft cries and pleas urged him on. Flooded with the need to give, he slipped his hand between her thighs.

When he thrust his fingers into her wet channel, he almost lost control. Clamping down on his response, he used his newfound knowledge. In seconds she came, crying out as she drenched his fingers.

Moisture pooled in his mouth. He was hungry for her. So hungry. Sliding down, he coaxed her to her back and feasted, loving her with his lips, his tongue and his teeth until she came again.

When the pressure in his groin bordered on pain, he finally left the bed and located the box he'd tossed to the floor. He rolled on the condom while drinking in the sight of Molly waiting for him.

She lay sprawled in the tangled covers, one slim leg dangling over the edge of the mattress, a seductive pose, an open invitation to make himself at home in the cradle of her body.

She watched him with the knowing smile of a woman who enjoyed the way he was looking at her, a woman who'd had a great time so far and was ready for more of the same. He couldn't wait to accommodate her.

It's never been this good, dude.

He pushed the concept away and climbed into bed with Molly. On his knees, he slid his hands under her hips and lifted. "Rest your legs on my arms."

She relaxed, opening herself to him.

Leaning forward, he pushed deep. Damn. He was going to come and there wasn't a thing he could do about it. He gasped as the climax hit him hard, sending tremors in both directions — to the top of his head and the bottoms of his feet.

He held onto Molly for dear life as the spasms shook him like a ragdoll. Throwing back his head, he let out a massive groan.

"Bret? Are you all right?"

"*Y-yes.*" He struggled to control his ragged breathing as he gradually stopped shaking. "I just..." He met her gaze. "Didn't mean to do that." Humbling.

"Well, that's a relief."

"Sorry. I didn't mean to scare you." He carefully disengaged. Easing her to the mattress, he left the bed and headed for the bathroom.

"I wasn't scared, exactly, just wanted to make sure you weren't having a heart attack or something," she called after him.

"Just an extremely forceful climax that took me by surprise." He disposed of the condom and washed up.

"I'm glad to find out you aren't always in control."

"I usually am, but not this time, obviously." He walked out of the bathroom. This time she was sitting up, facing in his direction.

"Because I make you crazy?"

He smiled. "Evidently. And I was hoping to give you another—"

"Oh, stop. I don't need any more. I've *never* had this much fun in bed." Then her eyes widened. "Um, I didn't mean that the way it sounded. Like I didn't have a good... because I did. *We* did. I wouldn't want you to think—"

"I don't." He walked over and sat at the foot of the mattress. "This was unexpected. That probably makes it seem more exciting."

"Right." She nodded. "I'm sure that's it."

"Could be the same's true for me. Like I said, this isn't my pattern."

"What is your pattern?"

"I'm used to going out with someone a few times, maybe spend the day with her at the ranch, meet her friends, have her meet mine, things like that." He wanted to touch her, hold her again, even if they didn't take it beyond that. But he didn't trust himself. She was tempting and they should call it a night.

"I don't really have a pattern. I met Aaron in college and he was my first lover." She looked straight at him. "You're my second."

That knocked him back. "I wish I'd known. I would've—"

"Treated me differently? If so, I'm *glad* you didn't know. The way you treated me was amazing."

"I never guessed you'd only been with one man. You made no secret that you wanted me, even though we'd agreed we have no business getting together."

"And we don't! But doggone it, Bret, you're sexy as hell."

He smiled. "So are you, Miss Molly."

"I never thought of myself that way."

"News flash, you're dynamite. We should put on our clothes and get out of here, but give me the word and I'll spend the rest of the night in this too-small bed making love to you."

"Thank you for that." She reached over and squeezed his shoulder. "But we need to get dressed so we can figure out what happens next. We've demonstrated that we lose focus when we're naked."

"I don't lose focus. I know exactly where my focus is."

Rivet scratched at the door.

He glanced at it. "I'm surprised she hasn't done that before."

"Oh, she has. You didn't notice and I didn't tell you."

He sighed. "Okay, time's up. We need to have a conversation." He retrieved her clothes from the floor next to the bed and handed them to her. Then he scooped up his. "Meet you out in the shop."

He opened the door and made it out before Rivet could get in. "Let her be, kitty-cat. She probably wants a chance to think, just like me."

But in the time it took him to dress, he hadn't come up with an answer. She could be the one. But she couldn't be the one. And he didn't do casual flings.

Even if he did, there was nothing casual about what had happened tonight.

10

Putting on clothes reminded Molly of the thrill of Bret taking them off. Every woman should have that kind of excitement once in her life. Well, she'd had that experience, and logic dictated she should end the relationship and call it good.

Bret couldn't be her next life partner because he never planned to live anywhere but Wagon Train. He might make a great dad for Zach and a willing participant in fathering Zach's sibling, but his ties to his family and this place ended the debate.

Even if she was tempted to keep having sex with him because it was awesome, and even if he broke his rule against casual affairs so they could continue giving each other pleasure, she'd be shirking her duty to find Zach a daddy. Irresponsible.

She could end things without telling him about Zach, but since that was one of her major concerns, not telling him didn't sit right with her. If they wouldn't be seeing each other except to coordinate the video project, he deserved to know her reasons.

Her game plan firmly in place, she opened the door. Bret stood about ten feet away cradling Rivet in his arms. She lay on her back, tummy exposed, a position no cat would take unless they completely trusted the person holding them.

Rivet was a cat, not a child, but Molly didn't have to see any more. Bret was a nurturer. It didn't change her decision to end the relationship, but it told her he was more likely to understand where she was coming from.

He glanced up. "As you can see, she's just a big old baby."

"Clearly. You said she's the shop cat. What about when you guys leave for the weekend? Who feeds her?"

"I take her home. Theoretically she's here to catch any mice that show up, but we rarely have a mouse. She'd get mighty hungry in two days, so she comes home with me."

"Gil never keeps her?"

"He will if I can't for some reason, but full disclosure, Rivet was my idea. Gil likes her, but he's more of a dog person."

And now she wanted to see Bret's place. She'd probably like it just as much as she liked him. But that made no sense, either. Time to cut and run.

She took a deep breath. "I've had a chance to think, and—"

"So have I." He set Rivet down and reached for her. "I don't want to end this." He drew her into his arms.

Dangerous place to be if she wanted to stick to her guns. "But you said—"

"I know what I said. I don't do affairs and you're not planning to stick around. But your grandmother told me to stop looking at the negatives and maybe she's right. You're here, now, and we have this chance to get to know each other. Why not explore that and see what happens?"

So tempting. The yearning in her heart nearly made her say yes. The light in his eyes told her he expected that answer. They wouldn't spend much time at Grammy's house, so she could keep Zach a secret the way she and Grammy had planned.

Except... she wouldn't be auditioning Bret for the role of Zach's daddy. She'd be taking advantage of Grammy's generous offer to babysit while she hunted for a husband.

She'd also be taking advantage of Bret. He was willing to risk a relationship in the hope that everything would somehow work out for them. But he didn't have enough information to make that call.

"You're not exactly jumping up and down with joy."

Swallowing a lump of misery, she slipped out of his arms. "It's a lovely idea, but I can't take you up on it." And maybe they could leave it at that.

"Why not?" Disappointment flickered in his amazing eyes. Then his chest heaved. "Are you having guilt feelings?"

"No. Well, yes, but not—"

"Judging from what you said, Aaron would want you to—"

"This isn't about Aaron. Well, it is in a way, but not how you're picturing it."

"Then how should I picture it? Because I'm totally confused. We just had great sex, at least from my perspective, and you seemed completely into it."

"I was." Her chest tightened. She dreaded telling him, but she had to. He wasn't going to just let her go, which meant he was already invested.

"I still think it has to do with you feeling disloyal. A while ago you got flustered after telling me it was the best—"

"I have a child."

"What?"

"A son. He's ten months old. His name is Zach."

He stared at her in disbelief. "Where is he?"

"Asleep in his crib at Grammy's house."

"At your *grandmother's*? Are you saying that while we were eating dinner, a *baby* was... wait a minute." His gaze narrowed. "That jingly ball. It's not a tambourine substitute."

"Zach likes to play with it under the table. She forgot to pick it up."

"What the hell, Molly?" His voice vibrated with anger. "What the hell's going on, here? Why the hell didn't you effing tell me?"

"Because..." Heat rose to her cheeks. It had sounded logical and smart when she and Grammy had concocted the scheme. "You weren't supposed to find out. You might have been a prospective daddy, but now I realize—"

"He's not Aaron's?"

"Of course he is! I promised Aaron I'd find a husband so Zach would have a father. It took a while before I could face the idea, but now that Grammy's offered to help, I'm determined to do it."

"Again, why not tell me about him? Especially if I was briefly in the running for that position?"

"I need to vet the guy before I reveal Zach's existence. Throwing a baby into the relationship right away would complicate things and make it harder for me to figure out if I've found the right person."

He studied her in silence for a moment. "I happen to agree with that."

"And it's not fair to Zach. He's reached the age where he gets attached. A parade of men through his life would confuse him."

His voice gentled. "You've given this a lot of thought."

"A lot more thought than I gave this incident tonight. Wonderful as it was, it doesn't fit the plan, so I can't see you anymore. I mean, I can *see* you, but I can't...."

"Have sex with me."

She nodded. "I'm grateful that we did, though, because I was afraid I'd have to force myself when the time came." She glanced at him. "Thank you for removing that particular worry."

"My—" He cleared this throat. "My pleasure." He paused. "Look, I hate to be a downer, but unless you're willing to marry some wet-behind-the-ears guy who's hankering for adventure, you'll have a tough time finding a husband prospect who wants to relocate to the big city."

She made a face. "I can't imagine choosing someone that young. I'm looking for steadiness and maturity, a man who'll be a good role model."

"I understand, but most of those are going to be like me and my brothers, firmly planted, working a job we like, looking to settle down here, not jaunt off to the big city."

"I can see that, now, but Grammy convinced me to come and think positive. Meanwhile she'll provide a rent-free place to live and a built-in babysitter."

"While you comb this little town searching for a needle in a haystack?"

She shrugged. "And catch my breath. It's been stressful thinking about what Aaron asked me to do, which really is the best thing for Zach, especially if I can find someone who's willing to have another baby with me as soon as possible, but I—" *Uh-oh.* "I didn't mean to tell you that part."

He studied her, his gaze unreadable. "It's an ambitious program."

"It was Aaron's and my plan all along. We were both only children and we wanted to have at least two kids, close together if possible. If he'd lived, we'd be trying again right now."

"Sometimes plans have to change."

"Clearly the timeline will, but I would like Zach to have a little brother or sister."

"I hope that works out." Bret shoved his hands in his pockets. "I guess that's it, then."

"You're upset and you have a right to be. But if I'd told you about Zach over dinner, would we have ended up in bed?"

He didn't answer right away. Then he met her gaze. "Probably not, and I wouldn't have missed it for the world."

Her breath caught. She'd tuck away those sweet words to savor later. "Neither would I. As to what I said afterward, you're right. I was flustered. I'd accidentally revealed something personal about Aaron and me. But the truth is, you're a better lover than he was."

Heat flickered in his eyes. "You were great, too."

"Until tonight, I didn't know I could be." She let out a sigh. "I guess you'd better take me home."

"Yes, ma'am."

11

Bret had to dig the truck out a little before they could leave. The snow had let up some, but it was still coming down and Main Street wouldn't be plowed for several hours.

He forged a path down the center, spraying snow like a speedboat on a lake. He prayed they wouldn't get stuck. The way this night was going, it was a distinct possibility.

"Do you think you can make it back to the ranch tonight?"

Her voice startled him. She hadn't spoken since they'd climbed in the truck, so they'd ridden in silence. He'd switched off the Christmas music because it didn't fit the change in circumstances. "I don't want to chance it. I'll just go back to the shop and sleep there."

"That bed is really too short for you."

"I didn't notice. I was too busy having good sex." It was an outrageous comment, but he was in a what-the-hell mood.

"Did you just make a joke?"

"Evidently not. You didn't laugh."

"I wasn't sure whether I should or not."

"If you weren't sure whether to laugh, then it wasn't much of a joke."

"On the contrary, it was a brilliant joke. If I'd been feeling as loose as I was when we were having good sex, I would have totally laughed."

"Damn it, Molly, we found something special tonight. I thought I could just let it go, but I'm having trouble doing that."

"I'm sorry."

"It's not your fault. I'm a grown man. I knew we didn't have much of a shot, but I barreled ahead anyway."

"Don't be too hard on yourself. Grammy's parting words influenced you. She meant well, but sometimes she ignores the obvious pitfalls of a situation."

"She looks on the bright side and that's not a bad way to live. It's just disappointing when you think something's on the right track and bam! It all goes to hell."

"I gathered that from your reaction. You said hell several times in a row."

"That's what I was going through."

"Me, too. I came very close to accepting your offer and keeping my mouth shut about Zach."

"Really?"

"Yes, really. The prospect of having a bunch more of that amazing sex was so tempting."

"So why didn't you go that route? I almost wish you had. Ignorance is bliss and all that." He made the turn onto her street, going slow, mostly because of the weather, but partly because he wanted to stay in this cozy truck with her for as long as he could.

"Not telling you would have been dishonest, a selfish choice on my part that wouldn't be fair to you or Grammy. I need to concentrate on finding Zach's new daddy."

"You should put an ad in the Sentinel. Wanted: Exceptional male role model with a few miles on him who's eager to procreate and can't wait to leave Wagon Train."

"Don't mock. He could be out there."

"Guaranteed he won't be a cowboy."

"I don't need a cowboy."

"You say that, but you have recent evidence we make better lovers."

"I shouldn't have told you. Now I'll never hear the end of it."

"Guaranteed. I'll remind you often." Except she wouldn't be sticking around long enough to make it a standing joke between them. He hated that. He was way too hooked on Molly Dixon.

"Listen, Bret, you need to park your truck and stay at Grammy's."

"No way."

"The streets are treacherous and getting worse. You've had to fight the wheel several times."

"But I won each fight."

"The snow's coming down faster by the second. It's getting as bad as it was when we arrived at the shop."

"Not quite."

"If you don't stay at Grammy's, I'll lie awake wondering if you made it back to the shop in one piece. And if you made it through the door."

"I'll text you when I get there."

"And if you don't get there? What if the engine quits and you have to leave your truck and hike to the shop, and then it comes down so fast you lose your way and we find your frozen body in the morning?"

"Good Lord, woman. You have a grisly imagination."

"I absolutely do, and it'll work overtime if you head back alone. I won't sleep at all."

"I'm not staying at Mrs. J's house. I'll make it back, no problem." Which was true, but the idea of staying was beginning to grow on him. In the morning he could meet the mysterious Zach. Which was okay because he wasn't a prospective father. He was a friend of Mrs. J's.

"It would be easy-peasy for you to stay over. She has a room all made up for my folks. It's a king. Way better than a tiny daybed."

"When are your parents arriving?"

"Not any time soon, unfortunately. My Grandma Irene isn't well and they don't feel like they can leave her."

"That's too bad."

"It's disappointing for all of us, but stuff happens, right?"

"Yes, ma'am." She didn't complain about it, either, which he appreciated. "I'm getting the distinct impression this invitation to stay overnight doesn't include sharing a bed."

"You thought it did?"

"Worth asking. You can share mine."

"That's not on the table. Grammy's a free spirit, but I'm not comfortable getting jiggy with a guy in her house, even if it's you."

"She really likes me. She might be happy about it."

"Granted, she might. She grew up in the era of free love. But it wouldn't be right for us to keep this up. It doesn't facilitate my—"

"Your goals. I get it. But it's not like you've met any likely candidates in the time you've been here. Seems like until you do...."

"You don't know. I could meet him tomorrow."

"If that happens, I'd back off immediately."

"Hey, I might be a big-city girl, but I watch TV. I have some concept of how small towns work."

"What's that got to do with it?"

"In small towns, everybody minds everybody else's business. Word will get out that I'm involved with Bret McLintock and that'll kill my chances of attracting anybody else."

"Maybe so, but that might be for the best this time of year."

"What's wrong with this time of year?"

"It's a sentimental season. When you're surrounded by snowflakes, candy canes and mistletoe, it's easy to think you're in love. But then you come to your senses, hopefully before you've made a lifetime commitment."

"Sounds like you have personal experience with this syndrome."

"I do, and it was a near-miss. We weren't right for each other, but one thing we absolutely had in common was a love of Christmas. The sparkly lights and the scent of cinnamon and pine put us in the frame of mind where we started naming our future kids and drawing up floor plans for the house we'd build."

"What happened?"

"January. Cold, wet, and not a sparkly light or a sprig of holly to be found. Without that holiday cheer, our hot love affair cooled down fast. Good thing she recognized it about the same time I did. The split was mutual and cordial."

"You were lucky."

"So lucky. She's married now and has a baby on the way. They met the first part of April, before any spring growth had popped up. That was a good thing, because spring is another minefield. Christmas and spring — you don't want to go husband-hunting during either of those seasons."

"You're just saying that because you want me to postpone the husband hunt and have sex with you, instead."

"Well, there's that." He pulled up in front of Mrs. J's Victorian and left the motor running.

Molly turned in her seat. "Forgive me for pointing this out, but what you're suggesting sounds suspiciously like a fling."

He sighed. "It does, doesn't it?"

"Are you rethinking your anti-fling stance?"

Yes, fool that he was. Might as well come clean about his motives. "I don't want to stop having sex with you."

"That's why flings were invented."

"I'm aware."

"And you're not in favor because you're looking for Miss Right. You pretty much said so on the drive to the shop."

"But as we've established, Christmas is a bad time to look for Miss or Mr. Right. Besides, I said that before we'd had sex."

"And that changed your mind about flings?"

"It was the best sex I've ever had."

"Oh, come on Bret. You've had more partners and more experience than I have. Tonight can't be the best you've ever had."

"Which is why I didn't say it before. I figured you'd think it was a line, or something I felt obliged to say after you said it."

"Then you *are* suggesting a fling?"

"Looks like it."

She gazed at him. "I need to think, and I can't when you're sitting there looking at me like that."

That was good news. "I could turn my head away."

"That won't help much. I'd still want to jump your bones."

"Don't let me stop you."

She shook her head. "That day bed was awkward. This would be worse. We need to get inside."

"And fool around in the guest room?" His blood heated.

"We're not doing that."

"Spoilsport."

"We need to get inside before the storm gets any worse. Then you'll sleep in Grammy's guest room and I'll sleep in my mom's old room, which is also Zach's room."

That cooled his jets. "I guess most couples don't have a fling when there's a baby in the picture."

"Exactly. And I'm not asking Grammy to watch him while I'm off flinging with you."

Complicated situation. How could he... wait. Yeah, that could work. "We can't do much flinging for the next few days, anyway. I'll be making luminarias, you'll be working on the video and then there's the fair. But it's over at three on Sunday. What if we take Zach to the ranch for a visit?"

"Nice idea, but I'm trying to keep him on the downlow. Showing him off to your entire family doesn't sound like a wise decision."

"And I promise it would be fine. My family knows how to keep a secret."

"Well, then maybe. I'm sure Zach would enjoy it. But what does that have to do with a fling?"

"It's a workaround. Since we're not going to expect your grandmother to watch him, he'll be with us, and since you don't want him bonding with me, the ranch is a solution."

"I don't get it."

"He'll have so many people and so many fun things to do that I'll just be part of the big picture. My brother Beau has a four-month-old daughter. My mom loves babies. There should be at least one of our old cribs around."

"A crib? Are you—"

"My cabin has two bedrooms."

"Are you suggesting that we'll borrow a crib from your mom so you and I can spend the night together?"

"I believe I am." This plan had promise.

"With a woman you just met? Won't she have a fit?"

"No."

"But—"

"Just take my word for it. Mrs. J is a free spirit, but my mom gives that term a whole new meaning."

12

Molly decided to leave the camera and case in the truck for the night. An icy wind buffeted her as Bret helped her out and tucked her against his side for the short walk to the porch. She barely noticed the cold.

The prospect of somehow continuing a sexual relationship with this man generated so much heat it was a wonder the snow didn't melt beneath her feet. But could she do it without sabotaging the plan?

"Grammy's bedroom's downstairs," she murmured as she took the keyring from her coat pocket. "There are four more upstairs, but only the two in front are in use. We'll just sneak in and go straight upstairs. You go left, I'll go right."

"Got it." He wiped his boots on the mat.

"Don't worry about your boots. She has another absorbent rug inside."

"Right. I remember."

"No talking." Shoving the key in the lock, she turned the knob and slowly pushed open the door. Bells jingled merrily. Darn it. Grammy had hung them on the door to amuse Zach. Maybe she wouldn't hear them.

Bret came in close behind her, gently closed the door and clicked the deadbolt. The bells jingled again.

A small lamp on a table in the entry gave them enough light to hang up their coats and hats. Bret slipped off his boots and left them by the coat tree. She put her soggy shoes there, too. She already missed the cozy socks she'd left at the shop.

The grandfather clock ticking in the hallway was the only sound as Molly crept barefoot toward the stairs and motioned Bret to follow.

"What have we here?"

Molly screeched and spun around, smacking into Bret, who'd been close on her heels. "Grammy! You scared me to death."

Her grandmother, a red and green plaid bathrobe tied at her waist, looked pleased with herself. "That was the idea. I couldn't resist. Heard the jingle bells. Then the distinctive clump of boots coming off. Grabbed my robe and tiptoed out here." Pulling her glasses out of her robe pocket, she put them on. "I assume you two were going upstairs?"

Molly gulped. The scene eerily replicated one from her college days when she'd been caught sneaking Aaron into her dorm room after hours. "I was worried about Bret driving back. It's bad out there, so I invited him to take Mom and Dad's room. I hope that's—"

"This house is yours, too, sweetheart. Of course it's okay." She turned to Bret, her tone chipper. "Did you get the luminarias done?"

"We did." He cleared his throat. "Sorry we woke you."

"I'm glad you did." She gazed at him. "If you'd shown up in the morning before I'd put on my glasses, I'd have beaned you with a frying pan."

"Yes, ma'am. And rightly so."

She chuckled. "I'm kidding. My eyesight isn't that bad. I would have been startled, though. Way better for me to scare the pants off you two, figuratively speaking." She winked at him.

She knows. Molly's cheeks heated. "I got a ton of video footage tonight, too. We both worked very hard. Took a long time to get it all accomplished."

"I'm sure it did." Her attention remained on Bret, the corners of her mouth twitching like she was trying not to laugh. "Since you've been invited to spend the night, or what's left of it, I'll take a wild guess that Molly spilled the beans."

"I had to tell him."

"I suppose you did. A baby is tough to hide first thing in the morning. And speaking of that, we should all toddle off to bed. Morning comes early when you have a little one in the house."

"So true. G'night, Grammy." She gave her a hug.

"Goodnight, sweetheart. Glad you made it home okay."

"Goodnight, Mrs. J. I appreciate your hospitality."

"Goodnight, Bret. Thanks for keeping my girl safe."

"Always."

"That's my boy. See you in the morning."

She left and Molly started up the stairs. Bret's steady tread behind her was close, his body causing the air to shift, his breathing a familiar rhythm, his scent arousing.

"I think she knows." His voice was soft and intimate.

It gave her goosebumps. "She does, but she'll wait until she gets me alone to have it confirmed."

"What will you say?"

"That we got carried away and now we're evaluating the situation."

He took a breath. "I can live with that. I'm more invested in keeping her good opinion than I expected to be."

"Give yourself a break. You never would have suggested what happened tonight. It was much more my idea than yours."

"I'd call it our idea." He paused while she unlatched the baby gate at the top of the stairs.

"I keep this closed whenever Zach's up here. He can climb out of his crib, now, and I don't want to find out the hard way that he's learned how to get the bedroom door open."

"Understood." He took the last step and moved aside so she could refasten the gate. Then he slid an arm around her waist. "I'll be a perfect gentleman tonight, but I need a kiss before you go."

"You need more than that." Fitting her hips to his, she met his gaze.

His breath hitched. "I thought we weren't going to—"

"We're not. But you need to know where the bathroom is."

There was just enough light to see his teeth flash in a grin. "Back to basics. Where is it?"

"There's only one up here, at the end of the hall."

"We're sharing?"

"Yes. We need to coordinate."

"Got your phone?"

She pulled it out of the back pocket of her jeans. "Right here."

He took his out, too. "Here's my number. Text me."

She keyed his digits into her phone and sent him a message.

He read it. "*Sleep tight, don't let the bedbugs bite?* That's the best you can do?"

"It's a classic!"

"So's this."

She looked at her screen and smiled. "You're going to be sending me X-rated texts tonight?"

"Is that a problem?"

"I can take it. Can you?"

"Probably not." He tucked his phone away. "You get first dibs in the bathroom. Text me, either when you're through or when you want company."

"We're not doing it in Grammy's upstairs bathroom, either."

"I know that. Just keeping the home fires burning." He cinched her in tight. "Now, about that kiss."

"I thought you'd forgotten."

"Never." His lips claimed hers with an assurance of a man who knew his kiss was welcomed.

And oh, it was. His clever mouth had seduced her tonight and then had proceeded to ravish her in ways that still made her quiver with longing. She wanted more.

Her core tightened in response to the bold thrust of his tongue. When he gently squeezed her breast, he reignited the craving he'd thoroughly satisfied in that cramped daybed. What wonders could he create on a king-sized mattress?

She kissed him until she was gasping for air and her panties were drenched. She wriggled out of his arms. "That's it. I'm outta here."

He backed toward the guest room door, his breathing as ragged as hers. "For the record, I'm ready to snap."

"But you want Grammy to think well of you."

"And of myself." His chest heaved. "I'm a McLintock."

13

Waking in semi-darkness, cool air on his face and the rest of him toasty warm, Bret savored the aroma of bacon and coffee mingled with the faint scent of pine. The sound of women's voices and baby giggles nudged a memory.

Twenty-four years ago, December mornings had started like this at Rowdy Ranch. He was four that year and his little sister Angie was ten months, just like Zach.

Christmas was only days away and Bret would wake up every morning with that delicious prospect front and center. While his mom and Marybeth made breakfast and tended to Angie, Marybeth's husband Buck would supervise the older boys, making sure they completed their chores. Bret's job was getting his younger brothers up and dressed.

At three, Gil was pretty capable. The two-year-olds, not so much. Lucky, the adopted son, tried his best. Rance went the other way. Usually Bret and Gil would just sit on him until he promised to behave.

Speaking of Gil, he'd better let him know his whereabouts. His brother had mentioned stopping by the shop this morning to check on the luminaria situation.

Throwing back the covers, he picked up his phone from the bedside table and found a text from Molly.

I'm going to grab a shower before Zach wakes up. I'll make it quick.

He'd been dead to the world, hadn't heard the phone chime. To his surprise, he hadn't tossed and turned all night. Maybe a sound sleep was his reward for being so doggone virtuous.

His message to Gil was short and sweet. *The luminarias are done, I'm visiting Mrs. J. I'll explain later.*

He'd laid his clothes over the back of the rocker in the corner of the room. He could put them on and head downstairs, but after sweaty work and even sweatier sex, he was grubby. Mrs. J and Molly probably wouldn't object if he showered. They might even appreciate that he didn't stink.

Tugging on his briefs and Wranglers, he scooped up his shirt and put the plan into action. The moist air in the bathroom had the same scent he'd inhaled when he'd run his fingers through Molly's hair last night. She must have washed it this morning.

He borrowed some of her shampoo and after some inner debate, used her razor on his scruff. Clean clothes would have been nice, but it wasn't like he'd spend much time in yesterday's duds. A change of clothes waited for him at the shop.

Looking as presentable as he could under the circumstances, he stepped into the hall just as Molly started up the stairs.

"Wave bye-bye to Grammy. Wave bye-bye."

"Bye-bye, Zach." Mrs. J called from below. "Bye-bye."

He stayed where he was. They hadn't talked about how she'd introduce him to her son. Hadn't scripted this moment at all.

He was so out of practice dealing with tiny humans. He was getting more comfortable around Beau and Jess's baby daughter, but she couldn't motor around on her own yet.

This little guy was capable of independent movement, probably choosy about who he hung out with and who got the cold shoulder. Was he accepting of strangers? Or fearful and shy?

A wave of dizziness hit him. Whoops, he was holding his breath. He dragged in air and let it out. Noisy. Not quite Darth Vader, but close.

Holding Zach propped against her shoulder, Molly came into view. The dark-haired tot bounced in her arms while he cooed and flapped his pudgy hand at Mrs. J at the foot of the stairs.

Molly glanced down the hall and put on the brakes, her gaze colliding with his. Then she cupped the baby's nape in a protective gesture, as if to stop him from turning around.

Bret edged backward, prepared to duck into the bathroom if that was how she wanted to play this. But she shook her head. He paused. Took another breath.

"Oh, Zach, guess what?" Her cheerful tone hinted that something special was about to happen. "My new friend Bret woke up. He's such a sleepy-head!" She turned sideways so Zach had a better view.

The little boy stared, his rosebud mouth working. But nothing coming out.

"Hello, Zach." Sounded like he'd been gargling gravel. Clearing his throat, he tried again. "Good morning."

Zach's head whipped around toward his mom.

"It's okay, sweetie. He's a nice man. That's just his sleepy voice."

Slowly rotating to take another look, Zach pointed at him and babbled something.

Bret took that as permission to come forward. "I'm glad to meet you, too, buddy." The little guy's Christmas-red sleeper was decorated with dried bits of something he'd likely eaten. He had Molly's warm brown eyes and her wavy dark hair. Her late husband's genes had to be in there somewhere, but they weren't evident at this point.

Zach continued to point at him while he communicated rapidly in Swahili. Or Mandarin. Or Klingon.

"I agree with you, sport. I think you're onto something, there." He glanced at Molly. "What's the plan?"

She smiled. "I just figured out that you're a plan-loving person." She jiggled Zach, who still had a great deal to say.

"It takes one to know one. Does Zach always talk this much?"

"Yes. I predict he'll end up a college professor or a politician. As for a plan, mine is to change Zach's diaper and bring him back downstairs. When Grammy and I heard the shower running, she decided it was time to make your breakfast. I advise you to go eat it before it gets cold."

"Yes, ma'am." He focused on Zach. "Great meeting you, dude. I hope we can do this again some time." He waved. "Bye-bye."

Zach flapped his hand. Then his little tongue came out and he blew a raspberry, a slobbery one with bubbles.

Bret automatically blew one back.

The baby giggled, revealing one lone bottom tooth. Then he blew another raspberry.

"Just warning you, he can do this all day."

"Me, too." He returned fire. "I used to get my little sister going. We'd keep it up until somebody yelled at us."

She laughed. "Consider yourself yelled at. He needs to be changed and you need to get some breakfast."

"Yes, ma'am. I'll get the gate."

"Thanks."

"Bye, Zach." He blew one last raspberry in the baby's direction.

Zach gave it his all. His little mouth vibrated as a cascade of bubbles rolled down his chin.

"Well done, dude." Flashing him a quick thumbs-up, he fastened the gate and clattered down the stairs two at a time. The kid was adorable. Just like his mother.

As he made his way to the kitchen, the combined aroma of bacon, raisin toast, country fries and scrambled eggs made his stomach rumble. He'd likely get a side of questions with his breakfast, but Mrs. J deserved some answers.

She stood at the stove, a bib apron over her jeans and sweatshirt. Her casual style took some getting used to. Until last night's delivery of the tree, he'd only seen her dressed in a skirt and jacket or a pants suit.

"Good morning." He wanted to make sure she'd heard him since he was in his sock feet.

"Good morning to you." She glanced over her shoulder. "Your boots aren't quite dry. I checked."

"Thanks. I can handle damp boots. By the way, I looked out the bedroom window after I got up. I'll be happy to shovel your front walk before I leave."

"What a lovely offer! I accept."

"Breakfast smells great. What can I do?"

"Pour us each a cup of coffee while I dish you up. My mug's on the counter next to the one I got out for you."

"I see 'em." Hers said *My Grandma's Gorgeous* and his said *Don't Squat with Your Spurs On.* "One of Hank's?"

"Yessir. He collected anything with cowboy logic sayings on it."

"Was this one a random choice on your part?" He finished pouring the coffee and carried the mugs to the table.

"Not so random. It's the same sentiment as the one that says *Don't Shoot Yourself in the Foot.* Both were appropriate." She carried over a loaded plate and set it on one of the Christmas-themed placemats. "I like this one better."

"The warning might be several hours too late." He pulled out her chair and waited for her to settle in before he took his seat.

"I'm not referring to what happened at your shop. That doesn't surprise me in the least. You two were giving off sparks like crazy during dinner."

He sighed as he laid his napkin in his lap. "She gets to me. We have issues, but I can't seem to stay away, even when I know that's the right thing to do." He tucked into his breakfast.

"Then don't stay away. She clearly likes you."

"I like her, too." He pointed his fork at the plate. "This is delicious, Mrs. J. Thank you." He took another generous bite of the country fries.

"You're welcome. Anyway, I understand why you're not comfortable having sex here."

He stopped chewing. Not a comment he'd mentally prepared for.

"But I'm happy to babysit so you can spend a night at the ranch."

He almost choked. Chewing quickly, he swallowed. "That wouldn't be right. You volunteered to watch Zach while she looked for a new husband. I'm not the—"

"Hush. We don't know that, yet."

He laid his fork on his plate. "I do."

"Her move to the city isn't a done deal, Bret. Some viable alternatives might present themselves."

"They might. But… there's another issue."

"Oh?" Her gaze sharpened. "What?"

"It has to do with Zach."

She bristled like a protective mama bear. "He's a beautiful baby and if you have some hang-up about raising another man's child, I'll be extremely disappointed in you."

"That's not the problem."

"What is it?"

He took a deep breath. "It's something I decided years ago, something that's very important to me. I want to really get to know a woman before we have a child together."

She studied him for a moment. "That does sound like a deal-breaker."

"I'm afraid so."

"I guess it's no mystery why you feel that way."

"No, ma'am. I respect my mother's choices. I even understand why she made them. But I want something different for myself."

"Fair enough. Have you told Molly?"

"Doesn't seem necessary. We've blown right past her guidelines for finding Zach's new daddy, so I should be officially disqualified. Odds are that concern of mine doesn't ever need to be discussed."

"Except it shows you two are cut from the same cloth. That's why she cooked up the plan to keep Zach under wraps until she'd spent a decent amount of time with a prospective hubby."

"And that's smart. I hope she's able to get enough info to make that call. But practically speaking, she doesn't have a lot of time, especially in Wagon Train. The word about Zach will eventually get out."

"I know that. She does, too. To be honest, I don't think either one of us is super confident this will work as we'd hoped. But she made a promise, and she's determined to keep it."

"Big promise." He couldn't fault the guy. Must've been awful, knowing he was leaving Molly in the lurch. Aaron had probably thought he was doing the right—

"Do you believe that when two people are meant for each other, Fate will find a way to bring them together?"

His attention swung back to Mrs. J. "Full disclosure, on the way to the shop last night, Molly told me about you and Hank. It's a wonderful story, but to answer your question, no, I don't believe that."

"I'm not surprised. Then again, you don't have to. Fate has a way of working whether you believe in it or not. Now eat your food."

14

During the brief time Molly was in the bedroom changing Zach's diaper, she heard the steady hum of conversation in the kitchen but couldn't make out the words. For some reason, they weren't laughing.

She and Grammy had laughed quite a bit while they'd analyzed this new development. Clearly that wasn't the tone of this discussion.

She'd rather not walk in on a serious heart-to-heart between those two. On the other hand, she'd love to get some idea of what they were saying. If she stayed in the upstairs hallway and entertained Zach with the contents of his toybox, she'd have a shot at eavesdropping.

Cross-legged on the floor in front of the baby gate, she helped Zach with the stacking cups he loved so much. Parts of the conversation drifted up the stairs, just enough to tease her without giving her a narrative she could follow. Frustrating.

The emotional overtones came through loud and clear, though.

Grammy had started out sounding like her usual assertive self, but then she'd become more subdued. Bret's voice had gentled. He sounded almost regretful. This interaction wasn't making either of them particularly happy. Good thing she'd stayed upstairs.

When the non-stop flow of words gave way to occasional comments that sounded food related, she decided the coast was clear. Time to take Zach downstairs and pretend she had no idea they'd been hashing out their differences. How maddening that she didn't know what they were.

She made a production of helping Zach put the stacking cups back in the toybox. Someday soon she'd have a fulltime job and she wanted a kid who picked up after himself. That done, she scooped him up, unlocked the baby gate and headed for the kitchen.

Grammy sat at the table drinking coffee from her favorite mug, the one Molly had given her for her seventieth birthday. Bret had one of Grandpa Hank's cowboy logic mugs. His plate was almost empty.

"Well, look who's here!" Grammy smiled and held out her arms. "Come sit with me, Zach."

He went to her instantly. He'd gravitated to her from day one, as if guided by instinct to trust the elder member of the clan to look out for his best interests. He wasn't wrong.

Grammy held him on her lap and made sure her coffee mug was well out of reach. "Bret and I have been discussing the front walk. He's offered to shovel it before he leaves but I think we should all get out there, either to shovel or offer support."

"Absolutely." Molly wouldn't mind seeing that cowboy's muscles in action again. "I'll either help shovel or wrangle Zach. Grammy, I seem to remember you're a talented snow shoveler."

"I'm not bad, but you're the lady from Boston, where it's piled higher and deeper because the streets are so narrow. This is a chance for you to strut your stuff. I suspect you could put us all to shame."

"It's not a contest." Bret looked at them. "Is it?"

Grammy eyed him. "It could be. I have two shovels."

"Let's do it." Molly blamed Bret's aquamarine eyes for that outburst. Since she couldn't grab him and kiss the living daylights out of him, she needed an outlet for all that energy.

He looked over at Zach. "What do you think, buddy? Want to referee?"

Zach blew him a raspberry.

Bret gave him one right back. "Game on."

Ten minutes later, Grammy sat on the porch holding Zach. She'd asked Bret to bring up one of the folding rockers stored in the basement. He'd also located an old cross-country ski pole to mark the midpoint of the walkway.

When he won the coin toss, he chose to start from the street.

"Bad choice, McLintock," Molly called out as he plowed his way through the drifts to the end of the walk. "More snow down there."

"But you'll have the sun in your eyes."

"Sun's behind the clouds." Just then it broke through and created a glare from the snow that nearly blinded her. She shaded her eyes with her hand and turned to Grammy. "Do you have—"

"There's an old straw one on the shelf of my bedroom closet."

She dashed into the house, pulled off her rubber snow boots and located the battered hat. Cramming it on her head, she tugged the brim low, put on her boots and returned to the field of battle.

"Thanks for the hat."

"Looks great on you."

She grabbed her shovel. "I forgot to ask. What does the winner get?"

"The honor of putting the star on the top of the tree."

"But that won't work if Bret wins. He has to get back to the — oh, never mind. I'm gonna win." Taking her position at the foot of the steps, she called out to him. "Ready?"

"Ready!"

Grammy raised her voice. "On the count of three. One-two-three-go!"

Fired up by the sight of the cowboy standing at the end of the walk, Molly began to shovel like her life depended on it. Then she checked to see how her opponent was doing.

He hadn't started. Instead he leaned against his shovel, watching her. Backlit by the sun, he transformed into a golden fantasy. Mesmerizing.

And confusing. "Why aren't you shoveling?"

"Giving myself a handicap."

"What?"

He just smiled.

Oh, hell no. "You're gonna regret that, buster! You are so going down!" She shoveled even faster. She would show that arrogant, hot, extremely tempting cowboy! Snow flew to the left, snow flew to the right. She gasped for breath and kept going.

Almost there. She gave him a quick glance. Dammit! He'd caught up with her! Must. Not. Lose. She switched on the afterburners, becoming a blur of perpetual motion — thrust, throw, thrust, throw, thrust — her shovel clanged against his.

Breathing like a freight train, she straightened and met the glimmer of laughter in his eyes.

"Seems it's a tie, Miss Molly."

"A tie? We can't have a—"

"The marker's right there." He gestured toward the ski pole on his left. "We reached it at the same time."

"So you say." She turned around. "Grammy, he claims we tied. But I won, right?"

"I'm afraid not, honey. It's a tie. You'll have to share the job of putting on the star."

"But we're decorating the tree this morning. He needs to get back to the shop."

"Looks like we need to reschedule for tonight, assuming Bret can make the time."

"I can, and thanks for the invite, Mrs. J."

"And you'll come for dinner?"

"I'd love that."

"Excellent. Zach and I are going inside. Bret, if you could please take the rocker—"

"I'll put it in the basement. And the ski pole."

"Thank you, dear boy. Zach and I are going to have a lie-down. We're exhausted."

"See you tonight, Mrs. J."

Molly peered at him. "I thought you'd be making luminarias far into the night."

"I can take a break. Besides, I need to bring you some of those luminarias so you can finish the video. Might as well enjoy your grandmother's great cooking while I'm here."

"You do realize Grammy's wooing you?"

"I do and I'm willing to be wooed. Who could resist a chance to put the star on the top of the tree? That was a prize worth winning." He pulled the ski pole out of the snow.

"Did you hear her say that was the reward?"

"I did. I have excellent hearing. And good eyesight. My teeth are all mine, too."

"You're a sandbagger, Bret McLintock."

He grinned, showing off those perfect teeth. "Let's go fetch the rocker."

"Did I ever have a chance of beating you?" She fell into step beside him on the newly cleared walkway.

"Not really."

"You wouldn't have had it so easy if I'd been at my peak. I got soft living in an apartment in Denver. If you'd been up against the Boston me, it would have been a different story."

"Afraid not." He climbed the steps and left his wet shovel leaning against the railing.

She hurried up after him and put hers beside it. "You don't know that!"

"Yes, ma'am, I do. Would you please take this?" He handed her the ski pole. "I need two hands."

She waited while he folded up the rocker. "How can you say you'd beat me no matter what?"

"I'm in training all year." He held the door for her.

"All year?" She walked in and switched her snow boots for the slippers she'd left by the door. "But you don't have snow... oh, I get it. You have to clean out the barn."

"Exactly." He brought the rocker inside and closed the door. "Mucking out stalls requires a rake and a shovel. It's snow in the winter and mucking out stalls year-round." He wiped his boots on the mat. "I've been doing it since I was five."

"I certainly didn't figure *that* in." She looked at his broad shoulders with new respect. "You're right. I didn't understand that about you."

"I don't work in the barn as much as I used to when I lived in the big house, but I still pitch in."

"And keep in shape for shoveling."

"I thought about saying something, but you acted like you were itching for that contest and I hated to pour cold water on the idea."

"I probably wouldn't have believed you, anyway. I needed a live demonstration. And it was fun, even if I never had a chance." She headed for the kitchen, where the door to the basement was located.

"You did great, though. I'll bet you'd be good at mucking out stalls."

"Thanks, I think." Flipping on the basement light, she walked down the narrow staircase, holding the railing with one hand and the ski pole in the other.

"You don't want to try it?"

"Shoveling horse poop? It's never been a dream of mine." She found the spot where the skis and poles were kept and returned the one they'd used as a marker.

"You don't know what you're missing. It's like a moving meditation. I've worked through a lot of issues while mucking out stalls. Repetitive motion gets you in the right frame of mind." He laid the folded rocker on the stack of others waiting for the first thaw.

"I'll take your word for it." And here they were, alone in the basement. Not the most romantic spot in the world, but that didn't stop her from getting ideas.

Irresponsible ideas. He had a job to do, an order to deliver. She started for the stairs. "Don't let me keep you. I'm sure your customer is eager to pick up the luminarias you—"

He gripped her arm, halting her progress. "Keep me, Molly. Just for a minute. I didn't ask you to take the ski pole for no reason. You notice I didn't take it back."

"I wondered about that." She turned and nestled against his warm, solid strength. Lifting her chin, she met his gaze. "Champion shoveler that you are, you could have carried the pole and the chair, no problem."

"Thanks for going along with my plan." Pulling her close, he took off her hat and laid it on the stacked rockers. Then he set his next to it. "Promise you'll talk your grandmother out of that hat."

"Why?"

"I love how you look in it."

Her breath caught. The tenderness in his smile filled her with warmth that had something to do with hormones but mostly to do with her heart. That affectionate smile reached into places that had gone dormant in the past year and a half. "You have a crease in your hair." Reaching up, she combed her fingers through one side, smoothing it out.

"Hat hair." Cupping the back of her head, he gazed into her eyes. "It happens."

"I wanted to fix it last night, when we drove to the shop."

"Why didn't you?"

"I didn't know you well enough to touch you like that."

Heat flared in his eyes and his grip tightened. "I want you to touch me like that. I want you to touch me everywhere. I want to make love to you so much I can taste it."

A familiar ache spread from her core to her trembling body. "I want that, too, but—"

"Come home with me tonight."

She gasped. "Tonight?" *Breathe, girl.*

"After we decorate the tree. Your grandmother said she'd babysit."

"When... when did she say that?"

"When we talked this morning." He rubbed her back in slow circles. "She suggested we spend the night at my place. Not specifically tonight, but since she asked me to dinner..."

"You think that's why she did?" A whole night alone, in his bed, in his cabin. She shivered.

"Yes."

"What about the luminarias?"

"Let me worry about the luminarias."

The determination in his voice sent heat rushing through her body, melting what little resistance she had left. "Are you sure Grammy understands that we're not... that you're not..."

"A husband candidate? Yes. Does she think I will be? Yes, again. I made it clear that giving us time alone won't lead to wedding bells. She doesn't believe me."

Temptation pulled her in one direction. Her sense of fair play pulled her in the other, giving her the jitters. "Is it fair to take advantage of her stubborn conviction that we'll end up together?"

"I can't make that call. I'm selfish enough to say yes, but she's your grandmother. All I know is last night blew me away. If that's all we'll ever have, I'll learn to live with it. But... I want you, Molly. And I'm pretty sure you want me."

"I do. Last night was special for me, too. I just—"

"One night. We can test it out, see how it goes."

Her jitters turned into giggles. "Oh, I think we know how it will go."

He smiled. "I meant we'll see whether we're riddled with guilt because we're imposing on your grandmother."

"I need to talk with her. Let me do that. I'll text you."

"Okay. But you can talk until you're blue in the face and she won't change her tune. She's convinced we're in the hands of Fate, whether we realize it or not."

He was right about Grammy. She took a shaky breath. "Okay. I'll come home with you."

"Thank you." He exhaled. "I was prepared for a no, but… thank you."

"You'd better get going, though."

"In a minute." He lowered his head and captured her mouth. Dark, rich passion flowed from his lips to hers. His tongue left no doubt as to his intentions when they were alone in his cabin, in his big bed, with hours to spare.

Cupping her bottom with both hands, he pressed her close. The imprint of his body against hers lasted long after he'd driven away. He would give her a night to remember. She couldn't wait.

15

"Are you out of your ever-loving mind?" Gil paced the length of the shop, waving his arms for emphasis. In the family, he was known as the drama king. They blamed it on the touch of red in his hair. "Don't you know a trap when you see one?"

"Mrs. J might think she's setting a trap, but Molly and I won't fall into it."

"Oh, right. Because your brain is operating at full power. That's always how it is when a guy thinks with his dick." He scooped Rivet up and hung her around his neck like a feather boa. "Rivet knows what I'm saying, don'cha, Riv?"

The calico purred as Gil gently rubbed her forehead.

"Rivet likes Molly."

"So what? I'll probably like Molly. She has great marketing ideas. But taking her back to your place when you've known her less than twenty-four-hours worries me, bro. It's out of character."

"A little, maybe, but—"

"A lot. Let's review. Two humongous red flags. She's not settling here and she has a kid. If you had the brains of a flea, you'd cut and run. Instead you're getting in deeper."

"It'll be fine. I've been burned by a Christmas romance so I know what to watch out for. So does Molly. If we start going in that direction, one of us will know it and pull the other one back."

Gil rolled his eyes. "I can just picture that as a fail-safe." He switched to falsetto. *"Oh, no, Bret, we're falling in love! Run away, run away!"*

"You're ridiculous."

"No, *you're* ridiculous. You can't convince me this relationship is all about sex. That's not who you are. You'll get invested."

"I won't let myself."

"So when it's over, it's over? You'll have no lingering feelings of tenderness for Molly, no haunting moments of regret?"

"Tenderness? Sure. Regrets? No. I'm going into this with my eyes wide open."

"Sure you are." He hunched down so Rivet could jump to one of the welding tables.

"She is, too. I'm not the one she wants."

"On the contrary. Hopping into that crappy day bed indicates a very motivated woman."

"I mean I'm not the kind of guy she's looking for long-term."

"Which is?"

"An urban type like her late husband. She was a hotel manager in Denver. She'll have to move to a bigger place than Wagon Train to get a job like the one she had."

"And you won't go running after her with tears in your eyes?"

"I'm not you, Gil."

"I only did that once."

"Besides, she's not the one for me, either."

"I dunno, bro. I can tell you're into her, whether you admit it or not. I think there's a real possibility that you'll get carried away and ditch that vow you made. That we both made. For good reason."

"Have you told anybody about that?"

Gil shook his head. "Have you?"

"Mrs. J, this morning."

"I'd hate for Mom to find out we feel that way."

"She won't."

"I hope she doesn't. Because on the surface it sounds like we're being critical of her. Speaking for myself, I'm not."

"Me, either. She's given us a great life."

"That's for sure." Gil smiled. "Couldn't ask for better."

"Nope." That smile was like looking in a mirror. Gil had the same nose as he did, and the same ears, compliments of their dad. "Remember when we used to sit on Rance to make him behave?"

He grinned. "Sometimes I still get that urge."

"Waking up in Mrs. J's house this morning with Zach downstairs making baby noises made me think about that Christmas when Angie was his age."

"Didn't Dad show up that Christmas?"

"Or the year after. I'm not sure."

"He gave us lariats. I still couldn't do much with mine. Except tie up Rance."

"At least he got us something to play with instead of clothes." He paused. "We sure did want Mom to marry him."

"Would've been a disaster, but we didn't know."

"Why in hell would a best-selling author hang out with a guy who never cracks a book, a guy who gets all his info and entertainment from TV?"

"Clearly she liked him, though. We're the living proof."

"Think about that. No other dad fathered a second kid. I'm grateful. I got you out of the deal. But why was he the exception?"

"Well...." Gil waggled his eyebrows. "There's one obvious answer."

He made a face.

"Don't knock it." Gil laughed. "That could explain why we're a couple of studs."

He snorted. "Yeah, right."

"My current theory is she never really wanted a husband. Just babies."

"Could be. She likes being in control of things. I don't see her sharing that control."

Gil shrugged. "And at the end of the day, it's her life. Her choice." He paused. "I'm not going to talk you out of taking Molly to your place tonight, am I?"

"Did you honestly think you could?"

"No, but I wanted to register my dissenting opinion."

"Duly noted."

"Then I'll drop it. For now."

"Thank God. So—the luminarias—you're in?"

"So in. I can't support your personal decisions regarding Molly, but going along with her idea to use luminarias as a promo? Brilliant, especially for our first year at the Christmas craft fair. The video's a smart move, too. Wish I'd thought of it."

"You'll help me make them?"

"Let's tuck Rivet in the back room and fire up those torches. Maybe you'll be so tired at the end of the day you won't have the energy for sex."

"Uh, that reminds me. Could I have the rest of that box? I'll replace it tomorrow."

Gil gave him a smirk. "What if I say no?"

"Then I'll have to—"

"Just kidding. I'd say take it with my blessing, but you don't have my blessing, so just take it."

"Are you going back to the ranch after we finish tonight?"

"I plan to. Aren't you?"

"I'd rather use the time to make more luminarias. I can shower and change here and go straight over to Mrs. J's."

"That does make more sense." He started laughing. "And since I'm going back, you want me to drop the box off at your place?"

"If you wouldn't mind. Taking it with me isn't exactly—"

"Smooth?" Gil was enjoying this way too much.

"No, but if you're going to turn this into a three-act play, I'll take the damn box and figure out a subtle way to—"

"Never mind. I'll deliver it to your cabin on my way home."

"Thank you."

"Did you leave a light on?"

"Not inside. The Christmas lights on the porch are on a timer, but none of my lamps inside are."

"Then it'll be dark in your house, and that's not welcoming."

"Do you care?"

"You're right, I don't. I'll just leave the box on that little table by the door and be on my way."

"By the door?"

"I'm not going to stumble around in the dark so I can put it in your bedside table drawer, your lordship."

"Oh. Good point. Then yes, please turn on a light in the living room and in the bedroom, so you can put the box in the drawer."

"Okay."

"And now that I'm thinking about it...."

"Yes?"

"I haven't been home since yesterday morning. I'd appreciate it if you'd do a quick pass — stick any dirty dishes in the dishwasher, make sure I didn't leave socks on the floor... you know what I mean."

"Absolutely. I'll take care of it."

* * *

A box of six luminarias on the passenger seat, along with the box of votives that hadn't been used the night before, Bret drove the short distance to Mrs. J's house, anticipation fizzing in his chest like he'd had too much to drink.

Molly had texted him around noon to set the time for dinner. He was going to be early. His crazy brother, despite being against tonight's activities, had offered to feed Rivet and tidy up the shop.

Bret had decided to go along with that, even though he'd intended to stay and do it himself. Everything Gil said or did came from a place of love and affection. He'd idolized Bret when they were younger, and that had morphed into mutual respect. Gil would go to the mat for him.

It worked both ways. Bret respected and admired his younger brother. If he ever needed anything, he had only to ask.

Gil's advice about Molly hadn't fallen on deaf ears, either. He'd told himself the same things. So why was he pulling up in front of Mrs. J's decorated Victorian, his heart thumping because soon he'd lay eyes on Molly in a few minutes?

Maybe he was just like his mother, who'd ignored the obvious incompatibility of the man she'd chosen to be her next baby-daddy. She simply hadn't been able to resist him.

He hadn't wanted to think about the reason his parents had connected, and then reconnected a year later. Maybe he should. It was a human reason, and God knows he was human, too. His strong attraction to Molly wasn't convenient. It didn't fit into his future.

But it loomed large in his present.

Striding up the shoveled walk with the box of luminarias and the candles, he gave himself grace for having illogical urges. Would a stronger man resist? No telling. He wasn't that iron-willed man, and it was okay.

16

According to Molly's plan, Zach would be tucked in and asleep by the time Bret arrived. Clearly Zach didn't care for that plan.

While Grammy put the finishing touches on dinner, Molly tried all the tricks she'd learned in the past few months. She sang to him. She rubbed his back. She sat in the rocker and set up a slow, soothing rhythm.

No dice.

Maybe he was teething again. She put numbing gel on his gums, gave him his pacifier and walked away from the crib.

Before she could make it to the door, he pulled himself up and started shaking the crib.

She tugged her phone from her pocket. Ten minutes before Bret was due. Grammy had started the Christmas music. "Okay, baby boy. Let's take a stroll down the hall." Lifting him out, she made the circuit while singing along with Bing Crosby's *White Christmas.*

Normally he drifted right off to sleep with this routine. But tonight wasn't normal, was it? She might want to blame teething or an upset tummy, but she was the culprit. Her body hummed with anticipation. Zach had picked up on it.

She'd almost asked Grammy to put him to bed for this very reason. But Grammy was busy in the kitchen and shouldn't have to stop what she was doing because her granddaughter had the jitters.

Zach gradually relaxed. His sturdy little body grew heavier. Another minute of walking him might—

The doorbell chimed. Her pulse leaped and Zach jerked awake. Grammy didn't have a lot of visitors, but he'd learned what that doorbell signified. Bret's deep baritone drifted up the stairs.

Zach twisted in her arms, pointed in that direction and started his litany of *ba-ba-ma-ma* interspersed with little crows of delight. Didn't take a genius to figure out he couldn't wait to see the big man who would play the raspberry game with him.

Neither could she, for entirely different reasons. "Okay, you win, son." She propped him against her hip, opened the baby gate and started down the stairs.

Bret stood in the entry talking with Grammy as he took off his coat and hat. His broad shoulders made the space look smaller and more feminine. A box of luminarias sat on the floor. He glanced up. "Did I wake him?"

"No." She broke eye contact before his mesmerizing gaze made her trip. "I haven't been able to get him to sleep. Then he heard you come in and he got excited. I think he recognizes your voice, now."

He frowned. "Is that a bad—"

"Oh, for heaven's sake." Grammy's gaze swept over the three of them. "I understand your worry that he'll bond and all that, but he gets excited about the pizza boy."

Molly relaxed a little. "He does. I think it's because he knows that soon he'll get a crust to gnaw on."

Glancing at the door, Zach pointed and babbled some more.

Bret smiled. "I think he understood most of what you said and he's looking for the pizza guy."

"I made hot rolls to go with the stew," Grammy said. "He can have one of those. Let's bring in his highchair from the kitchen so he can sit with us."

"I'll do that." Bret followed her down the hall.

Bouncing in her arms, Zach blew a raspberry at his retreating back.

"I think he missed that one, son."

"Did not," Bret called over his shoulder. "Catch you later, sport."

What a sweet moment between a kind man and a little boy. Could that be why Zach lit up when Bret was around? And the pizza boy?

Her son was used to female voices—her girlfriends in Denver and now Grammy. Except for a couple of visits from her mom and dad, he'd rarely had a chance to hear a male voice except in short snatches. Maybe Bret's baritone was music to his ears.

And to hers. She'd been drawn to his magical gaze, but his voice had played a part in those first few moments at the Christmas tree lot. No getting around it. She had a huge crush.

He continued to feed that crush as he pitched in to get Zach set up. Crouching beside the dining table, he laid down the oilcloth Grammy used for a fall-out zone under the highchair.

"This is a staple in our family, too." He smoothed it out. "Or was. It'll probably be a thing again when my niece is ready for a highchair."

He had nice ears. She hadn't noticed that before. "What's her name?"

"Maverick." He stood and lifted the wooden highchair onto the oilcloth.

"Maverick?" She managed to keep track of the conversation and still make time to admire the flex of muscles under his white shirt and the snug fit of his wear-softened jeans. Good thing she could multi-task.

"My brother Beau loved the name but he had to work on Jess before she'd agree to it." Unlatching the tray, he pulled it forward. "I wondered if I'd remember how to do that. Guess it's not something you forget."

He smelled delicious, too, like cinnamon. Whatever he used as an aftershave suited him perfectly. "But aren't highchairs all different?" She settled Zach in and pushed the tray into place.

Her son gazed upward in silence, his focus moving from her to Bret and back again.

"Guess they are all different. This one's like the one we have."

Zach continued to stare at them in obvious fascination, his rosy lips parted.

What was going through his head? She reached out and ruffled his dark curls.

"He looks like you."

His soft comment sent a shiver of pleasure down her spine. She gazed into his eyes, more green than blue tonight. "I'll take that as a compliment. He's a cute kid."

He smiled. "I meant it the other way around. You're beautiful. He's a lucky guy."

"Oh." His words sank in slowly, warming all her secret places. "Thank you."

His eyes darkened and he raised his hand as if to cup her cheek.

"The stew is dished! Come and get it!" Grammy called from the kitchen.

Stopping in mid-motion, he gestured toward the kitchen door instead. "After you."

As she walked ahead of him, his compliment added a sway to her hips. The hitch in his breath was subtle, but it jacked up her anticipation another notch. How long would it take to eat? How long to decorate the tree?

Stay in the moment.

Grammy had shoved her glasses to the top of her head. Lowering them, she peered at her. "Are you okay, sweetie? You look a little flushed."

"I'm fine, Grammy."

The concern in her eyes turned to a look of understanding. Smiling, she handed over two potholders. "Use these. The bowls are hot."

Not as hot as the cowboy standing behind me. She turned around and he stepped aside to let her pass.

Earlier she'd helped Grammy set the table. Before taking Zach to bed, she'd put out the salads, her contribution to the meal. She'd never been drawn to food prep, and a career in the hospitality industry had given her access to restaurants. She and Aaron had eaten out more than they'd cooked.

Bret's enthusiasm for homemade food was alluring, though. Sensual. Sexy. Cooking a meal with him would be a whole new experience. No telling whether she'd ever have that opportunity, but she'd grab the chance if it came.

Grammy chose the head of the table, which put Zach's highchair on her right and Bret on her left. Molly sat next to Zach so she could monitor him. It also gave her an excellent view of Bret.

He'd chosen a glass of red wine instead of beer. "It's good," he said after an experimental sip. "Mom and the Wenches drink wine but I never developed a taste for it. I like this one, though."

"Hank liked it, too, although only for a change of pace. Beer's a cowboy classic." Grammy handed Zach another roll after he'd shredded the first one. "I admire the cowboy who'll try a glass of wine, instead of automatically choosing his manly-man brew."

"In that case, you have permission to serve me wine from here on out."

"It doesn't count if you're kissing up, Bret. In fact, you lose points."

"Then I'm losing 'em right and left." He grinned at her. "I've been kissing up ever since I arrived."

"Then you're not as smart as I thought. You don't have to curry favor with me."

"Why not?"

"I've been your biggest fan ever since you checked out *War and Peace.* I think you were around nine."

Molly blinked. "Did you read it?"

"I tried. I barely got past the first chapter." He glanced at Grammy. "Sorry, Mrs. J. If you've built my reputation on *War and Peace,* I'm probably down a truckload of points by now."

"I didn't expect you to read it. But you checked it out. That took cojones." She winked at Molly. "Isn't that a great word? So much more elegant than... the one most people use."

"Yep." But she couldn't think about either word now or she was liable to combust. She turned to Bret. "What made you think you should read *War and Peace*?"

"The Wenches used to reference that book all the time. Mom didn't have a copy, so I went to the library. When I saw it was a big sucker, I decided to check it out just to see the look on Mrs. J's face when I smacked it down on the counter."

"And made her a fan for life."

"Yeah, that surprises me. I'm not sure why."

"I admire your style." She gazed at him with fondness. "You're not flashy, but you have a subtle way of making people take notice."

You said it, Grammy.

"Now you're making me blush."

"One time I had to refuse to let you check out a book. Remember?"

"I do."

"Okay, I'll bite. What book wouldn't Grammy let you have?"

"*Lady Chatterley's Lover*."

"Oh!" She took a sip of wine. "Well, now. Were you still nine?"

"Eleven."

He'd developed an interest early. No wonder he was so good at that activity. Her insides squeezed, just a little, reminding her how good.

"The Wenches talked about that one, too. They didn't know how much I eavesdropped."

"Did you ever read it?" Grammy tucked into her stew.

"Finally got my hands on it when I was thirteen. Mom had a copy but wouldn't give it to me until then."

It was an arousing subject best left alone, but Molly's curiosity got the better of her. "What did you think?"

"I loved every word, except the parts I didn't understand, so I got my brother Sky to explain those. He was a worldly eighteen."

Okay, enough. They needed a segue to a topic that wouldn't send her up in flames. But what?

"I think we're boring Zach." Bret chuckled. "He looks like he wants to challenge me to a spit-fest."

Or maybe Bret and her son would save her from herself. Zach had abandoned his mangled roll and sat staring across the table at Bret. His rosebud mouth was working, and every so often his tongue would peek out.

Grammy cracked up. "He so *is* challenging you, Bret! It's High Noon all over again!"

"I hate to spoil the fun for you two, but he's always sticking his tongue out, giving it some air. It's what he does."

"I believe that, except for the past few minutes he's been totally focused on me. We do have a history. But if you want me to ignore him, I will."

"*I* don't want you to ignore him." Grammy put down her wine glass. "Let Bret do it, Molly. I want to see this raspberry face-off. Take a video on your phone."

"Are you serious?"

"C'mon. It'll be funny as hell."

She turned to Bret. "I'm sure you don't want—"

"I don't care. Just don't add it to the one you're making for the fair."

She laughed. "No worries."

"Then go for it. And send me a copy."

"Okay, then." She took out her phone and switched to the chair at the opposite end of the table. "Are you loaded and ready?"

"Yes, ma'am."

"Zach, are you loaded and ready?"

As if he'd understood every word, her son puffed out his chest and blew a loud raspberry in

Bret's direction. Then he giggled and clapped his hands. Bret was laughing so hard he almost didn't manage to send one back. But he did, and they were off, trading raspberries.

How Bret managed to keep going without cracking up was a mystery. She tried to control her own laughter for the sake of the video, but it was a lost cause. Grammy laughed until the tears came.

When Bret finally called a halt, he stood, reached across the table and shook Zach's pudgy little hand. Zach wasn't finished, though. He added one last raspberry, chortling and smacking the wooden tray with both hands.

Molly caught Bret's big grin and his thumbs-up. Then she stopped the video. "It's a wrap."

Grammy took off her glasses and wiped her eyes. "Indeed." She gazed down the length of the table and gave Molly a subtle nod.

It might have been in reference to ending the video, but Molly knew better. Bret's willingness to act like a goofball with her son had just won him a bunch of points. As if he needed them. In Grammy's mind, the search for Zach's daddy was officially over.

17

After dinner, Molly took Zach upstairs to tuck him in, leaving Bret alone with Mrs. J. When she pushed back her chair, he stood and automatically started collecting dishes.

She gave him a glance of approval. "Your mom raised you right." Grabbing the cloth napkins and the wine glasses, she led the way into the kitchen.

"She had to with such a big family. We were each expected to do our part."

"That's a built-in bonus of having a lot of children. Hank and I had planned on having more kids, but when it didn't happen, we just concentrated on the one child we had and made sure we didn't spoil her rotten."

"I'm sure you didn't." He set the dishes on the counter. "Want me to load the dishwasher?"

"That's a sweet offer, but since they're my dishes and my dishwasher, I can do it faster. I left the lights and ornaments in the parlor by the tree. You could go start testing the lights for me."

"Be glad to." He started to leave the kitchen.

"But before you go..."

Turning back, he met her gaze. Chances were good she wanted to comment on his interaction with Zach.

She didn't disappoint. "You're great with that little boy."

"I like him. He's a kick."

"He likes you, too."

"That's not the issue. Or maybe it is. He's a scene stealer. Most kids are. They demand attention one way or the other."

"I understand your position. I do. But I look at you and Molly and I see a glowing future."

"I'm not denying we have chemistry, but we barely know each other. And with Zach around, we can't make a lot of progress there."

"Which is why—"

"It's not enough."

"It could be. Over time."

He started to say it. Changed his mind. Molly and Zach were temporary residents, but Mrs. J hadn't faced that.

"Don't you find yourself wanting to get to know her? Don't deny it because I can tell you do."

"Sure I want to get to know her. She's terrific, but—"

"So true." Molly breezed into the kitchen. "I am terrific. Zach's asleep."

"Already?" He glanced at her. "That was fast."

"He was exhausted from blowing all those raspberries. But you two seem to have stalled out, here."

"We got to talking," Grammy said.

"About me." She glanced at him. "Or rather, about us."

"Yes, but we need to get this show on the road," Mrs. J said. "I feel a little guilty keeping you two here, but I really would like to get the tree decorated and it's... large."

"Grammy, that's my doing. I wouldn't dream of leaving it all to you."

"Good, because even with the big stepladder I couldn't put the star on the top. Anyway, go on in and I'll finish up here. The lights need to be untangled and tested. And if you'd like a fire, you're welcome to build one."

"We're on it, Mrs. J." Bret followed Molly out of the kitchen. Walking behind her was turning into one of his favorite things. She'd added a little hip motion to her walk recently. He liked it. A lot.

She glanced over her shoulder as she walked through the dining room and into the parlor. "I'll build the fire if you want to start on the lights."

"Nice try. I distinctly heard your grandmother use the word *untangle*."

"She wasn't herself when she put those lights away. Grandpa Hank wasn't well and I think she knew it would be their last Christmas. She was frazzled."

"Ah. I get it. Probably would have been easier to just get new lights."

"I suggested that but tossing perfectly good lights just because they're tangled didn't sit well with her."

He sighed. "She's right. It's wasteful. I just... let's build the fire together and untangle the lights together. How's that?"

"Nice idea, but this fireplace is small. It's more of a one-person job." She walked over and moved the grate aside.

She had a point. He should tackle those lights. "It can be a two-person job."

"How?"

"You crouch in front of it and I'll hand you stuff."

She smiled. "This is a compact area. I can get to the newspaper, kindling and wood box, no problem. I don't need an assistant."

"Work with me, here, Molly. I purely hate untangling Christmas lights." And he'd use any excuse if it meant being near her.

"Aww, poor baby. I'd hate to see you cry." She hunkered down on the hearth, reached in and opened the flue.

He crouched next to her and breathed in her scent. Some of the dinner conversation had aroused her. He could tell. "I wouldn't *cry.*"

"Sure sounds like it. Newspaper, please." She held out her hand.

He gave her a whole section of the *Sentinel.*

"Hel-*lo.* One sheet at a time so I can crumple it up." She handed it back.

"Sorry. I know better." He peeled off one sheet. "Your grandmother's impressed with how well I get along with Zach." He separated out another sheet.

"She's impressed and I'm worried." She stuffed the crumpled newspaper under the grate.

"I shouldn't have played the raspberry game at dinner." He handed over another sheet.

"How could you help it? He was acting adorable and Grammy wanted to see it. I don't blame you. I just—"

"I know." He handed her one more sheet.

"That should do it. Kindling next."

"I find it's better if you put that on top."

She looked at him and frowned. "Kindling? On top of the logs?"

"Yeah, try it. Put the logs on and then the kindling."

She narrowed her eyes, clearly skeptical.

He wanted to kiss her so much. He restrained the impulse. "Trust me."

"Okay. Logs."

Evaluating the size, he gave her a couple of good-sized ones for the bottom and then some smaller ones. She stacked them exactly as he would have. He chose not to mention it. Didn't want to sound patronizing.

He handed over two more small pieces. "Now the kindling." Picking up a fistful of sticks, he passed them to her.

"I can't believe this works."

He gave her another bundle of sticks. "It will if you prime the flue."

"What? I've never heard that."

He twisted a piece of newspaper into a shape that would act like a torch. "Light the top of this and wave it around in the chimney area. It warms it up, gets it more receptive to the fire."

"You made that up. You're just trying to get me hot."

"I wasn't, but if I'm doing it accidentally, props to me. Did I get you hot?"

"I'll neither confirm nor deny." She lit the coil of newspaper.

"Which means I did."

"Not necessarily." She waved the flame inside the firebox. "Am I doing this right?"

'Stick it up a little deeper into the chimney. You'll get a better response when you light the fire."

"Hey, McLintock. That was deliberate."

He chuckled. "What?"

"You know what. Is that enough?"

"Should be. Now light the newspaper under the grate."

"The big test." She touched the flame to the crumpled paper and sat back on her heels. "I could make a fortune if I put that raspberry video online."

"Do it without my permission and I'll sue the pants off you."

"That's an expensive way to get my pants off. You strike me as a man who's clever enough to accomplish that without getting lawyers involved."

He looked over at her. "Is that a challenge?"

"Not much of one, I'm afraid." She gazed into the fire. "When you get that gleam in your eye, I'm ready to strip down."

He gulped. "I think I just miscalculated."

"Jeans getting a little tight, are they?"

"Yes, ma'am, and now I have to stand without groaning." He evaluated the situation with the logs. "Fire's burning real good, though."

"Yes, yes, it is. Your method is stellar. Now you can't get up without pain and my panties are drenched. Was it your brilliant idea to build this fire together?"

"If we'd been alone, it would have worked out perfectly." He pushed himself to his feet and clenched his jaw against the pain in his privates. Once they made it to his place, he'd suggest ditching their clothes until they headed back to town in the morning.

"Ready to untangle some lights?"

"I must have failed to mention how much I dislike doing that."

"Oh, you mentioned it. But you've enjoyed two amazing meals Grammy cooked, mostly with you in mind. And she's babysitting Zach for the whole night, so we can—"

"'Nuff said. She's more than earned her right to call the shots." He walked toward two snarled balls of Christmas lights snuggled next to each other on the floor. "She's got some cojones, though."

Molly lost it. Cute as hell. She was still giggling when her grandmother showed up carrying a step ladder and a large shopping bag from Miller's Hardware.

Leaning the ladder propped against the nearest wingback chair, Mrs. J looked at Molly. "What's so funny?"

Gulping, she gestured toward the two balls of Christmas lights. "Cojones."

"Oh." She studied them. "They do look like giant ones, don't they? Well, I have a surprise for you kids. I left them here because I thought untangling them would be a good exercise to find out if you were as compatible as I think you are, but—"

"Grammy!" Molly was still hiccupping from her fit of laughing. "You set this up as a test?"

"I did, but then this afternoon I changed my mind. While Zach was napping and you were working on the video, I went shopping." She held up the bag. "New lights."

"Great news, Mrs. J. Thank you."

"They were even on sale."

"Even better." Instead of wrestling with two mangled balls of lights for at least an hour, he'd have more time for loving Molly.

"Thanks, Grammy." She gave her a hug. "Ready to put them on?"

"I'd rather turn that over to you guys, if that's okay."

"Well, sure, but—"

"I'll hang the ornaments once we get to that stage, but the fire you made looks inviting. I'd rather sit and watch you two handle the lights and the garland."

Bret was onto her, now. "Is it another test?"

"No, no." She settled into a wingback chair that gave her a view of the fire and the tree. "Somewhere I read that if you really want to get to know someone, find out how they deal with tangled Christmas lights. I decided to try it."

"Bret's already informed me he hates doing that, so I predict he would be a pain in the ass." Molly handed him one of the boxes of multicolored lights.

"Not in front of my biggest fan."

"I wouldn't be the one watching. I would have stayed in the kitchen and listened to see if either of you started cussing."

"I would have cussed softly."

"My hearing's still excellent."

"Is that right?" Whoops. Had she heard—

"Interesting fire-building technique. I'll have to try it sometime."

Yep, she'd likely heard it all. Time to redirect the conversation. "I freely admit I don't like tedious jobs. Molly could be the soul of patience. I guess we lost the chance to find out."

"I hate tedious jobs, too." She took a box out of the bag and handed it to him. "How are you on stringing lights?"

"That I enjoy." He opened the flap and pulled out the string of lights, twist-tied into two sections. "If there's an outlet... ah, I see one under the windowsill. If we start from the bottom, we can test strands as we go up."

Molly picked up another box. "How else would you do it?"

"You can start at the top, testing each strand as you go."

"That's not very efficient."

"I agree, but we have to make sure we don't run out of lights before we get to the top."

She set down the bag, pulled out the boxes and stacked them. "That's what we have to work with."

He studied them, looked at the tree and glanced over at Mrs. J. "Good eye."

"This isn't my first rodeo, cowboy."

"Clearly. Let's do this, Molly." He crouched down, plugged in the first string, looped it halfway around the bottom branches and handed the rest to her. "It'll probably only go around once."

"My thought, too." She handed him a second string.

Sure enough, he had to reach across the back of the tree and grab the end so he could connect the two. They kept up the routine, handing sections of lights back and forth until he had to get the stepladder.

At that point, his height and long arms came in handy. Molly gave him the last string and it was exactly long enough to end at the top, where the star would go.

She gazed up at him. "Perfect."

"Sure is. I could put the star on while I'm up here."

"You could, but that's not how we normally do it. We get everything on and then do the star last."

"Us, too. Just checking. How about the garland?"

"That we can do top to bottom. I'll hand it up to you."

When she gave it to him, he started arranging it the way his mom liked it. "How's that?"

"Great. Keep going."

He finished the part that needed the ladder and they worked together on the rest. Standing back, he surveyed the tree, moved forward and adjusted one section of the lights.

Molly fiddled with the garland some more and stepped away. "Looks fantastic."

"Just how I pictured it would."

"Me, too." She turned toward her grandmother. "What do you think?"

"I think I just gathered a whole bunch more evidence."

Uh-oh. Bret had a hunch what was coming. *Don't take the bait, Molly.*

But she did. "Evidence?"

"It's as plain as the nose on your face, honey. You're made for each other."

18

Molly loved her grandmother to pieces but she had to quit saying stuff like that. "I know you believe in Fate and all that, but—"

"It's not only Fate, sweetheart. It's common sense."

"You're kidding, right?" She glanced over at Bret, who rolled his eyes.

"I saw that look. You think I'm crazy as a bedbug."

"I don't think you're crazy, Grammy. You just have unrealistic expectations."

"There's nothing unrealistic about it. I'm not counting on some New Age mystical force to bring you together. That might have happened last night when you fell in love with that tree, but I'm talking about cold, hard facts."

"Like what?"

"I've known you all your life. I've known him ever since he was old enough to get a library card."

"I don't see what that has to do with—"

"Hear me out. I know your mother like the back of my hand. She's been married to your dad for twenty-nine years, so I know him pretty darn well, too. Bret's family isn't as familiar as my own, but we've lived in the same town and had a friendly relationship since before he was born."

"And?"

"When I say you and Bret would get along like grits and gravy, I have a solid basis for making that claim."

"Because you know both families?"

"Yes, ma'am. You grew up in different parts of the country, but you share a set of values. You were each raised with love. You know how to love another person."

Bret waded in. "Even if that's true, we haven't had time to find that out. Won't have time. It takes months. Years."

"He's right, Grammy."

Her grandmother smiled. "If you say so." She stood. "I promise not to bring it up again. How about some Christmas cookies and coffee while we put on the ornaments?"

"Love some," Bret said. "Mom always brings out Christmas cookies when we decorate the tree."

"Mine, too." Molly gave him a startled glance. Then she shrugged. "I'm sure lots of families do that." Grammy had messed with her head. Now she'd be seeing similarities every time she turned around.

* * *

"So we're actually going to do this thing." Now that Molly was listening to Christmas music in Bret's cobalt blue truck on the two-lane highway that would take them to Rowdy Ranch, she had jumping beans in her stomach.

"If memory serves, we've already done this thing. Twice."

She glanced at him. The glow from the dash revealed a dent in his freshly shaven cheek. He was smiling. "I suppose you're not the least bit nervous."

"Oh, I'm nervous, all right."

"You don't look it."

"Cowboys work hard on that. We're the strong, silent type. We don't let people see us sweat."

"Are you serious?"

"I'm kidding. Mostly."

"I hope so. It's healthy to show emotion. There's nothing wrong with manly tears."

"Mom's tried her best to convince us of that but I can count on one hand the number of times I've seen one of my brothers cry. Not counting when they were babies, of course."

"What about your sister?"

"Come to think of it, she's not a crier, either."

"But your mom is?"

He laughed. "That's the irony. She's the least tearful woman I've ever met. When she's mad she'll scorch your ears with salty language, but she won't cry. She broke down when Angie's dad died in a rollover. That's about the only time I remember."

"I'd like to meet her."

"Tonight?"

"God, no. Sometime. Does she know anything about this?"

"By *this,* do you mean—"

"Me spending the night out here with you."

"She does not."

"Good."

"I don't think."

"What do you mean *you don't think*?"

"Gil knows, but I can't imagine why he'd tell her about it. On the other hand, I didn't specifically say not to. Probably should have, huh?"

The jumping beans were back at it. "Is he likely to tell her?"

"Not really. It's not like him to go blabbing to Mom. And he has no reason to see anybody else. Unless he drops by Beau's place to find out how Maverick is doing. Or he might check on those pigs. Ever since Maverick was born, we've all—"

"Pigs? What pigs?"

"Beau has two pot-bellied pigs. We all love Slim and Pickens."

"Cute names." Would Gil spread the word? Did she care? Maybe not so much about his brothers.

"Those pigs have a heated shed out behind the cabin. Should be fine, but Beau's a new dad. Discombobulated. So we check on 'em."

"Beau's family or the pigs?"

"Both."

"Are you saying Gil might have stopped by to check on either your niece or Beau's pigs, and in the course of that visit, he might have mentioned that I would be spending the night at your house?"

"It's possible. Probably not, though."

"And he knows about Zach?"

"Yes."

"Oh, well, we talked about bringing him out here, anyway."

"Yes, ma'am."

"I'm rethinking my original plan to keep him a secret. It's too complicated and it's not fair to him. He needs to socialize, hear male voices."

"Bringing him to the ranch will accomplish that, and like I said, my family won't say anything."

"I believe you, but I should take him into town, let him see how pretty it looks all decorated."

"And take him to see Santa Claus?"

"Probably not."

"It's his first Christmas. Don't you want a picture of him with Santa?"

"He won't understand what's going on. It's not like he'll ask Santa what he wants for Christmas."

"The Santa visit isn't for Zach. It's for you, so you can have a picture in the album of him sitting on Santa's lap wearing a cute outfit, like an elf, maybe. That's the outfit Beau and Jess found at the Baby Barn for Maverick's picture with Santa."

The album. Every new mother was supposed to have one. She didn't. Random shots on her phone, yes. And now that hysterical video of Bret trading raspberries with her son.

But an official album of Zach's first year didn't exist. It could be cobbled together, but it wasn't available for viewing this very minute.

"You're quiet over there."

"You reminded me of an area I've neglected."

"You haven't started an album for Zach?"

"No."

"I figured that was the case since you clammed up the minute I mentioned it."

"I have a lot of just him, and some of him with my friends, but it felt weird taking selfies all the time, so I stopped. If you have another parent, then you can trade off — pictures of baby with his dad, pictures of baby with his mom."

"I could help you create something. If you dig back through the pictures on your phone, you probably have more good ones than you think."

His offer charmed her. He had no future with her or her son, but he clearly wanted to do this. "Capped off with a Santa picture?"

"That was my thought. Then you could take it from there."

"This seems important to you. How come?"

"We each have an album. Well, except Sky. That's a long story. But the rest of us have one, complete with pictures of our dad. Mom didn't end up with any of them, but she wanted us to have a record."

"Now I *really* want to meet your mother. She sounds like a very unusual lady."

"She charts her own path, that's for sure."

"How soon before we get to your cabin?"

"About five minutes."

Her pulse skyrocketed. "Now I'm nervous again. Are you?"

"You bet."

"You have no reason to be. You were amazing."

"That's why. You said I was the best ever. Where does a guy go from there? You can't improve on the best ever."

Her heart melted. How many men would admit they were worried about such a thing? His honesty soothed her jangled nerves

She wanted to do the same thing for him. "Last night we were virtual strangers. We know each other better, now. We have more time." She smiled. "And more space."

"There's that."

"I see lights. Is that your cabin?"

"Yes, ma'am."

"It looks so homey with the lights on inside and the Christmas lights on the porch railing. Do you have a tree?"

"I don't. I kept thinking I'd have time to cut one, but then I agreed to that luminaria order. And now I still don't have time."

"After the fair?"

"It'll be the eighteenth already. Is it worth it?"

"Of course it is! Did you say you cut your own?"

"I always do. But this year was so different, with the metalworking business taking off like it has."

"Going into the forest and choosing a tree would be so cool."

He pulled up in front of the cabin and shut off the motor. "You've never done it?"

"Nope."

"Okay, then. Unless we get another snow on Sunday, we'll make an expedition of it after the fair. And take Zach."

"That would be awesome. Thank you."

"Ready to go in?"

She met his gaze and her heart lurched. The night before she'd been on fire, desperate, a little crazy for the hot, talented artist she barely knew but had to have.

This was different. More personal. Tonight she craved the man who'd played a silly game with her son, the man who hated untangling Christmas lights, the man who'd offered to help her make a baby album for Zach.

Tonight she'd make love to Bret McLintock.

19

Gil had been right about turning on lights inside. The cabin showed off a lot better that way. Bret wanted Molly to like his place, although that made no sense at all.

He helped her out, his heart pounding as he led her toward the porch steps. A whole night. In a king-sized bed. Made him dizzy. And hot. So hot.

Had he swept the steps after the snow? Nope. Gil must have. What a guy. He'd be sure to thank him.

Molly's snow boots were better than her shoes from the previous night, but because of Gil's efforts, he didn't have to worry she'd lose her footing on a patch of ice.

She paused at the base of the steps. "Aw, you have a wreath on the door. It's gorgeous."

"Compliments of Buck and Marybeth." He started up the steps. "They make them for us now that we each have our own place."

"Buck and Marybeth?"

"Oh, right. You wouldn't know. Mom hired them years ago. Buck's our foreman and Marybeth helps Mom with the house. And us when we were younger."

"So that's how she managed."

"Yes, ma'am. They're part of our family, now."

"Nice."

"Sure is." He crossed the porch and reached for the doorknob.

"You don't need a key?"

"Hardly ever lock it. Don't need to." He opened the door and stepped back to let her go in first. "Welcome to... aw, hell."

"Oh, my goodness!"

"I'm gonna kill my brother."

"I thought you didn't have a Christmas tree." Molly giggled as she wiped her boots on the mat and walked inside.

"I don't have a Christmas tree." He stomped on the mat, wishing it was Gil's face. "But I do have a brother whose days are numbered." He came in and shut the door. Six feet away stood the small entry table that usually sat to one side, a convenient spot for tossing keys, mail and loose change.

Tonight it held none of that. Instead, a table-top Christmas tree sat on it with red, green, silver and gold condom packets hanging from every branch, the foil reflecting the beam from a small spotlight mounted over the door. So many condoms.

Molly gulped back laughter. "At least we won't run out."

"I should have known, dammit. No wonder he was willing to...." He trailed off.

She glanced at him, her dark eyes sparkling. "Willing to do what?"

"Um..." Oh, what the heck. "This plan was last minute, and I didn't have any..."

"Condoms at home?" She grinned at him.

"I did not. I was short on time to buy some, plus I didn't want to walk into the cabin with a box of condoms in my jacket pocket. Not classy."

She started laughing again. "Ah, but this." She gestured toward the tree. "This is the height of sophistication."

"Like I said, my little brother is doomed."

"I'm guessing you asked him to drop off what was left from last night."

"Yes, ma'am."

"But these aren't from that box."

"I'm aware of that."

"He went to some trouble." Another giggle popped out.

"That's what worries me. Stay here while I make a sweep. I don't want any more surprises."

"Okay." She pulled her phone from her coat pocket. "Can I take some pictures while you're gone?"

"You want a picture of that?"

"Who knows if I'll ever see anything like it again?" She glanced at him. "Do you mind?"

Did he? No. If the picture made the rounds, he'd come off as a stud who needed an unlimited supply. "Just don't put it online."

"I won't. This is for my personal record."

"Of what?"

She blinked. "My life in Wagon Train, I guess."

"Oh. Sure, go ahead. I'll be back in a minute." He headed down the hall toward his bedroom, the next likely place for some Gil sabotage.

Molly's response about the picture had hit him like a cold shower. Maybe he was misinterpreting, but a photographic collection titled *My Life in Wagon Train* sounded like a segment from a much broader picture, like his town was a whistle stop on her way to somewhere else.

Which it was, right? He'd figured that out twenty-four hours ago. And he was fine with it. He wasn't her ideal partner and she wasn't his.

Both bedside lamps were on their lowest setting. Just how he would have done it. The covers were turned back and the pillows fluffed.

A note in Gil's handwriting was propped against the lamp nearest to the door.

You're probably cussing me out right now, bro, but face it, you left me an opening a mile wide. I remembered Rance had bought a whole bunch of Christmas-themed condoms. Just like him, right? I talked him out of them, but only because I promised you wouldn't use any. I can't imagine how he figures he'll need all of these between now and New Year's, but the boy has high hopes. Anyway, you can keep the tree, but not the little raincoats. The ones from the shop are in your bedside table drawer. We didn't plant any other surprises. Enjoy your evening.

Bret opened the drawer. The sight of those foil packages brought back the moment he'd put the first one on last night, when he'd been out of his mind with good old-fashioned lust. His cock swelled.

Tossing the note in the drawer, he left the room and unbuttoned his jacket on the way down the hall. Enough of this nonsense.

Molly's coat and red scarf hung on one of the horseshoe wall hooks mounted near the door. She'd left her snow boots by the front door and she stood in her sock feet near the tree, still taking pictures.

Without her boots, wearing only socks on her feet, she looked comfortable and relaxed. Completely at home.

He'd had several women in this cabin over the years. Each one had been attractive, personable and, ever so slightly out of place. Molly was not.

"Bret, these condoms are hysterical." Turning to him, she held up one she'd removed from a branch. "The foil's a solid color on one side and imprinted with a holiday item on the other. This one's red on one side and has a candy cane on the other."

The candy cane image took him straight to a different image, one that made his jeans pinch. That was the other thing about Miss Molly. She got him hot faster than any woman he'd dated. "We can't use them."

Her eyes widened. "We can't? Why not?"

"Gil left me a note saying they're just for the effect."

"But if we can't use these—"

"It's not a problem." Fighting the urge to just grab her, he crossed the room, took off his jacket and hung it beside her coat. He put his hat on the next hook over. "He left the ones from the shop in my bedside table drawer. We're covered." Which was about the time his sense of humor kicked in. "So to speak."

"Why can't we use these?"

"Because they're on loan." He closed the short distance and slid his arms around her waist. "Just to create the effect. We can look but we can't open."

"Well, that's no fun."

"I agree." She smelled so great. Felt even better. "Let's go find some that we're free to open."

"Good idea." She tossed the condom onto the table. "Are these Gil's, then?"

"No." Might as well answer her questions before they got into the good stuff. He didn't want to talk about his brothers once they were naked. "They belong to my brother Rance."

"Why does he want them all back? Surely he doesn't expect to use—"

"Gil said Rance has high hopes." So did he, that in a few moments they'd leave this episode behind them.

"Does he think a Christmas wreath on the wrapper will seal the deal?"

"Maybe it will. You seem to like them." Drawing her close, he let the exchange of body heat work its magic. The last of his irritation with Gil and

Rance evaporated as the steady thrum of desire claimed him.

"They make me laugh." She nestled against him and wound her arms around his neck. "That doesn't mean I'd go to bed with some guy because he had a holiday-themed condom in his pocket."

"Good thing, since these are off limits for me."

"I think Rance wasted his money."

"Evidently he believes they'll work in his favor since he wants us to give them all back."

"*Us*? Does that mean I get to be there when you return them?"

He laughed. "Do you want to be?"

"Oh, yes, yes I do."

"Then I'll make that happen." He gazed into her expressive eyes. The view never got old, especially when they were stretched out, skin to skin. "Can we leave the subject for now?"

"Probably should."

His grip tightened. "This isn't how I expected tonight would go."

"Me, either. I thought first you'd give me a tour of your house."

"Do you want one?"

"Well, I had a chance to look at your living room while you were gone. I've never been in a modern log cabin and I like the peeled log effect. The rock fireplace is beautiful and the furniture looks comfy."

"Thanks." He would maneuver her over to the couch, except the essential item was in his bedside table drawer. "The kitchen's through there." He tilted his head in that direction. "I don't have a dining room. Do you want to see—"

"Maybe later." She snuggled closer, a promising sign. "How about showing me your bedroom?"

Heat traveled directly to his groin and set up permanent residence. "I thought you'd never ask."

20

The persistent ache of longing had bedeviled Molly ever since walking into this fantasy log cabin owned by a man she couldn't resist. Visions of his king-sized bed waiting down the hall wouldn't leave her in peace.

Finally, she was on her way to making use of that wide expanse of mattress. Thanks to last night's excellent beginning, she had confidence in the outcome. Bret knew how to do things right.

When they reached the doorway, he let go of her hand. "Here we are. Make yourself at home."

She peeked inside and sucked in a breath. He'd doubled down on the log-cabin coziness of the living room. The rustic bedframe and nightstands looked handmade. So did the quilt, which went on for miles.

Without stopping to consider what would be a cool or appropriate move, she dashed into the room, launched herself onto the bed and rolled to her back. Propping herself on her elbows, she met his amused gaze. "Come and get me, cowboy."

His eyes glittered. "Yes, ma'am."

Before she could catch her breath, he'd ditched his boots and climbed onto the bed. He went for her jeans, first, stripping them off along with her panties and flinging them aside.

His urgency fed right into her fantasy and sent moisture to all her significant places. She undid the buttons on her shirt to help things along. Surely he'd want that off, too, and her bra.

Or not. Leaning over, he pulled out the bedside table drawer and tossed her a condom.

She blinked. "But you're not even un—"

"Open it for me?" He reached for his belt buckle.

"Yessir." Heart pounding, she tore the wrapper. The clank of his belt buckle and the buzz of his zipper told her all she needed to know. This was happening.

He shoved his briefs and jeans down and took the condom. "Thanks."

She was treated to a brief glimpse of his magnificent equipment before he secured the condom and sank deep into her quivering channel. She let out a long, heartfelt sigh.

"Good?"

She glanced up, gulping in air. "Oh, yeah."

"Lie back. Let me love you."

Sinking onto the soft quilt, she reached up and gripped his shoulders. "You're still wearing your shirt."

"So are you." Breathing hard, he began to stroke. "Next time... next time we'll... we'll get everything off."

She arched into the rocking motion of his hips. "I don't care."

"Didn't think you would." His chuckle was low and intimate. "Not when you issued that sexy invitation."

"I did?"

"*Come and get me, cowboy?* What did you suppose would happen?"

"I don't know."

"This, lady." He pumped faster. "This is what happens."

"I'll..." She gulped as her core tightened. "I'll keep that in mind."

"Is it what you wanted?"

"Yes." Her climax arrived, plunging her over the waterfall into the swirling waters below. "*Yes.*" The rapids took her, spinning and tossing her in the dizzying sensations that left her gasping.

He slowed the pace, moving more deliberately. He dragged in a breath. "You got to me."

Opening her eyes, she met the intensity in his. "Seems like... you got to me."

He smiled. "Didn't mean for it to be quite this... abrupt. But you... I couldn't...."

"Help yourself?"

"Yes, ma'am." He pushed in deep and stayed there while he took long, slow breaths. "When you want me like that, it's powerful. A force of nature, as they say."

"But it doesn't make you want to come?"

"Yes, but the drive to give you an orgasm is stronger. It's a quest. Never mind about the niceties. I just want our significant parts available so I can give you what you need."

"That sounds like the mating behavior of some exotic animal narrated on a wildlife video. Assuming the creature being studied is doing the talking, which they never are, but still."

He laughed. "Okay, I'm being too dramatic."

"No, you're not! I like it. What happens between us has a primitive vibe. That's one of the things that makes it so exciting." She cupped his tight buns. "But you need excitement, too, buster. Your turn."

"I like hanging out here, tucked in, watching the way your eyes get bright when you're ready to come and go all mellow after you do. I'm in no hurry to come, unless I'm overstaying my welcome."

"Not at all. I'm just saying that if you give in to the urge to come, which has to be nagging at you, then we can move on to... other options."

"Like what?"

"Oh, like the idea I had when I looked at the Christmas condom that had a candy cane on it. I used to love those as a kid, especially the big thick ones."

"Hmm. Interesting."

"Why?"

"I wonder if it was the same idea I had when you mentioned candy canes."

"Lean down and I'll whisper my idea in your ear." She could just tell him straight out, but murmuring it seemed way more erotic.

Lowering his head, he put his ear within whispering range.

She cupped the back of his head and put her mouth very close, so her warm breath would go into his ear as she described in detail what she had in mind for him.

His breathing quickened. The part of him linked intimately with her gave a twitch. And he began to move, slowly at first, but quickly gaining speed.

Then he shifted position, angling his strokes so he reached the sweet spot that guaranteed she'd travel this road with him. And he borrowed her idea.

Putting his mouth close to her ear, he began describing all the ways he'd give her pleasure tonight. His hot words blended with his rapid thrusts until she was taut as a drawn bow, reaching... reaching... *there.*

She abandoned herself to the glory of it, letting the full-throated cries come, holding nothing back as her body bucked and trembled.

"*Good.*" His voice was raw as he pounded into her. With a hoarse bellow, he drove in once more.

Powerful spasms rocked her core. She closed her eyes, relishing the feel of his climax, the sound of his heavy breathing. A drop of moisture fell on her cheek. And another.

He licked them away.

Opening her eyes, she looked into the warm blue of his gaze.

The corners of his eyes crinkled as he smiled. "How're you doing, there, Miss Molly?"

"Couldn't be better."

"Me, either. Got a little hot and sweaty, though. I'm thinking a shower would be nice. Care to join me?"

"Great idea."

"I have more where that came from."

She laughed. "No doubt."

"Give me a couple of minutes to take care of this condom." He eased away from her. "There's nothing even slightly romantic about these things."

"A necessary evil."

"Yes, ma'am." He left the bed and kicked off his jeans and briefs before ducking through the door into the bathroom.

Condoms. Not a lot of fun, even dressed up in special Christmas packages. She and Aaron had been so eager to have kids they'd ditched birth control a couple months before the wedding.

She hadn't conceived right away, so she'd enjoyed sex without condoms for a couple of years. Bret was just plain better at it, even with a condom. Without one? Likely off the charts.

Too bad she'd never find out.

21

Bret believed in condoms. His whole family believed in them. Except for the time Beau had used one Jess's cat had chewed, they'd prevented countless unplanned pregnancies for the McLintock clan.

But tonight he resented the clumsiness of the process. Molly had called them a necessary evil. That nailed it. He had to use one, was grateful they existed, but they kept the experience from being all it could be. This recent episode with Molly had been spectacular, but he craved more.

If making love with her was this good with a condom, how great would it be without one? He wanted to know, dammit. And he never would. With Molly, anyway. Someday, with someone else... but the chances of finding someone as wonderful as—

He sucked in a breath. Enough of that. Unhelpful and depressing.

After divesting himself of the darn thing, he unbuttoned his shirt partway and pulled it off over his head. Then he took off his socks and threw his shirt and socks in the hamper. He'd worry about his jeans and briefs later.

"All clear?" Molly appeared in the doorway looking fetchingly naked.

"Just waiting for you, milady. Love the outfit."

"Love yours. We're matchy-matchy."

"I wouldn't say that." He deliberately ogled her full breasts. "I don't have a pair of those."

She gave his privates a once-over. "And I don't have a pair of those."

"True."

"Or that other thing."

"Yes, you do. It's just smaller. And hidden."

She smiled. "You've studied feminine anatomy."

"My favorite subject." He held out his hand. "Wanna be my lab partner?"

"You're a smooth talker, McLintock." She put her hand in his. "I'll have to be careful or I'm liable to end up flat on my back with my feet in the air."

"Would I do that?" He tugged her closer.

"I believe you promised to put me in that position, along with several others too shocking to say out loud."

"So you remember."

"Vividly."

He cradled the back of her head. "Here's one activity I failed to mention, and it's long overdue."

"What's that?"

"Kissing." Touching down gently, he savored that first electric contact, the first compelling taste. Then he settled in, exploring the lush contours of her mouth with his tongue, slackening his jaw so that she could return the favor.

She kissed the way she made love — all in. In seconds he was fondling, stroking, breathless and aroused. Ready again.

Gasping, he broke away. "Shower."

She put her hand to her heaving chest. "A cold one?"

"Hell, no. We're getting into a nice warm shower so we can continue what we've started."

Her eyes darkened. "That sounds good. Very good."

"It will be." Heading for the roomy shower stall, he pushed the left-hand slider open and turned the water on. He put his hand under the spray. Not warm yet.

She came up behind him and reached around, closing her fingers over his stiff cock. "I get to go first."

"No, you don't. I'll—"

"I insist." She tightened her grip.

"Easy does it."

"Ready to explode, are we?"

"Yes."

"Let me take the edge off. Then you can have your turn. I called it." She gave him a gentle squeeze. "Okay?"

He clenched his jaw against the urge to come. His gallantry was losing ground to the image of her mouth working on a thick peppermint stick. A guy could only be so noble. He caved. "Okay."

"Excellent." She released him. "Steam's pouring out of the shower. I think the water's hot."

He hadn't even noticed. He quickly turned down the temp so they wouldn't scald themselves, slid the glass door closed and opened the one on the far side. Shaking with anticipation, he gestured for her to step in.

"Big shower."

"Yes, ma'am."

"What's the tiled bench for?"

"When I'm old and infirm."

"What about when you're young and extremely firm?"

"Then I can use it... differently. Are you going in or not?"

"I am." She stepped over the lip, and when he joined her and closed the door, she reached for him.

He moved back. "Wait."

"Why?"

He grabbed a washcloth from a hanging shelf. "I need to scrub up."

"Oh. Right. It's been so long since... well, never mind." She plucked the washcloth from his hand. "Let me do the washing up. That'll be fun, too."

So long since she'd had sex that involved condoms? Only an idiot would envy a dead man, but for a split second, he did.

Then she began tenderly washing his very needy cock, and he gave thanks for being in this place, with this woman at this moment in time. He was a lucky guy. Even if she'd be gone in a few weeks, she was here now.

She was here and she was... ahhh. No more washcloth. Just her soft touch, teasing him with feathery strokes as she sank to her knees and started... licking. He groaned.

"Too much?"

"No. I mean, yes... I mean..." He took a shaky breath. "It's been... a while." *Why admit that, doofus?*

"Then it's about time."

Good. No questions.

"This will help." She gripped the base and squeezed.

Sure enough, the pressure to come eased a little. But only a little. When her warm mouth closed over the sensitive tip, he shuddered. Balled his hands into fists. Counted backward from a hundred.

Warm water sluiced over his shoulders and down his back. He tightened his glutes. *Delay. Delay.* He was so close. Didn't want it to end. Ever.

But when she grabbed his ass and got serious, he was out of time. Letting go with a massive groan that bounced off the tiled walls, he came and came hard. Good thing she had a grip on him with the way he was shaking.

He didn't black out, but he saw stars. She stayed with him, each swallow a subtle caress. No one had ever loved him better.

She released him tenderly, with butterfly kisses along the length of his extremely satisfied cock.

Opening his eyes, he dragged in a breath and looked down. "Thank you." He grasped her arms and drew her to her feet. "Best ever." Cupping her face in both hands, he kissed her, going deep, giving thanks.

She tilted her head back, wrapped her arms around his neck and pressed her slick body against his.

Closer. He needed to be closer. Sliding his hands down her back, he cupped her sweet bottom and lifted her so she could wind her legs around him. They fit like puzzle pieces.

He tightened his hold. Her moist heat tucked against his abs and her plump breasts cushioning his pecs fed a hunger more intense than he'd had for any woman.

Lowering her gently to the bench, he cradled a dewy breast in each hand, dropped to his knees and gave in to his craving. When her moans turned to urgent cries, he hooked his shoulders under her knees, dipped his head lower and gave her the climax she begged for. And another, because he didn't want to stop.

He might have tried for a third if the hot water hadn't run out. At first Molly didn't seem to notice so he kept going.

Then it turned icy and she let out a shriek.

He lifted his head. "Too cold?"

"Are you kidding?" She scrambled from the bench and was out of the shower before he'd managed to turn off the water. "That's like snow melt!"

"It gets like that in the winter if you let it run."

"Which is why I don't." She grabbed a towel and wrapped up in it. "Aren't you freezing?"

"Not exactly." He stepped out on the bathmat.

She glanced at his family jewels and smiled. "I see. I thought cold water was supposed to take care of that."

"It might have if I'd stood under it long enough, but I decided not to bother. Eventually it might go down on its own." He grabbed a towel and dried off. "One way or another."

"What way would you prefer?" She rubbed the towel over her head, leaving her hair looking wild.

He liked it. "What do you think?"

"I think you'd like another roll in the hay with yours truly."

"Sure, but if you're orgasmed out, then—"

"I probably am, but I'm impressed that you're still interested. That's flattering." She grinned. "Which makes me inclined to go along with the program." She hung up the towel. "Follow me, cowboy." She sauntered out of the bathroom.

Which he did, because he was totally hooked on Molly Dixon. Gil had warned him this would happen.

So he'd miss her like crazy when she left. He'd deal with it. In the meantime, he'd soak up all the Molly goodness he could.

22

Turned out Molly wasn't orgasmed out, after all. Bret was one potent cowboy. He delayed his climax while he made sure she was along for the ride, and then they came together, which was lovely.

After he took care of the condom, he came back and stood by the bed. "I'm not being a very good host. Can I get you something?"

She propped her head on her hand, enjoying the heck out of the view. "You've been a stellar host. I've had a super time so far."

"Nice to hear, but can I offer you something to eat or drink?"

"After Grammy's meal and sugar cookies, I definitely don't need something to eat, but I'd take something to drink."

"Apple cider?"

"A cold bottle of apple cider sounds delicious."

"Alcoholic or virgin?"

"Virgin, please."

"Be right back."

She took a mental picture of his naked backside as he left the room. He was a terrific guy and she'd like him even if he didn't have a cute butt, but the fact that he had one was a nice bonus. Also having goodies on the flip side added quite a bit to the pleasure of his company. He was the whole package. Ha, ha.

Since they were about to have a chat over a couple of drinks, she sat up and rearranged the pillows. He had four regular ones instead of two gigantic king-sized that supposedly went with such a bed. She preferred the smaller kind. Her head got lost on the oversized ones.

She propped two on his side against the headboard and two on her side. Her side *temporarily.* For tonight, anyway.

He walked in with two bottles dressed in crocheted sleeves, one Santa and one Rudolph. "Take your pick."

"Rudolph, please. I grew up with Rudolph. I wanted to ride a reindeer, or at least ride in a sleigh."

His eyes lit up. "You want a sleigh ride?"

"Does your ranch have one?"

"Brand-new this year. Christmas red. Mom bought a draft horse named Thor to pull it." He handed over her drink.

"I'm in. Can we take Zach?"

"Absolutely." He climbed into bed and settled back against the pillows. "Wouldn't dream of not including him. And your grandmother. We'll invite her, too."

"Our Sunday activities are mounting up. Cutting a tree, taking a sleigh ride, meeting your family...."

"Not so overwhelming. We could combine the sleigh ride with getting the tree, and you'll likely meet most of my family at the Christmas fair, so by Sunday you'll be old friends." He took a sip from his festively decorated bottle.

Cute. And endearing that he'd taken the time to add the crocheted sleeves. "So how will you introduce me to your family? What am I supposed to be? Not your girlfriend, exactly, but—"

"I'll introduce you as my friend. My family's observant. Even if the word hasn't gotten around by then, they'll pick up on our relationship. They can tell the difference between a friend and a *friend.*"

"Won't they be curious? Since we just met? I'm stitching all this together, but you said it had been a while, and—"

"Yes, I sure did." He sighed. "The Christmas romance that went wrong. But what a dumb thing for me to say in the middle of the action."

She couldn't help smiling. "In the middle of the action?" Glancing over, she caught his slight wince.

"Sexual relationships 101. Don't reference a previous relationship while engaging in the current one. *Especially* not during sex."

"Hey, don't worry about it. I did it, too, when you had to remind me about condom residue aftertaste. We're even."

He met her gaze. "Tell you what. We'll start with a clean slate. Our past history stays in the past. We'll concentrate on the here and now."

"Works for me." She reached for a new topic. "What's it like to grow up in a big family?"

"Great. Wouldn't change anything. It's been an amazing experience."

"Is that what you want, eventually?"

He tensed.

"Sorry. Two seconds ago we agreed to focus on the present, and I—"

"That's okay." Reaching over, he squeezed her thigh. "Sounded good at the time." He turned his head and met her gaze. "And I know why I said it. I like you. A lot. In the future... you're not there."

"I know." The truth hurt. "I like you a lot, too. You're so good with Zach. I can see you being a wonderful dad, but that might not be your—"

"Oh, it is." He was silent for a while. "I don't see myself with ten kids. But I want some. At least two. I agree with you on the only child thing. But... I wouldn't want them right away."

"Oh?" Her chest tightened.

He hesitated, took a breath. "I want time to settle into the marriage. Get to know each other. Before... before we have kids."

She gulped. Did Grammy know this? How could she and still believe that—

"I didn't mention it before because—"

"You know I'll be leaving." She turned to him. "Why mention it now?"

"Tell me if I'm wrong. But I think maybe... maybe you're starting to—"

"I'm not." Her voice quivered, but she kept going. "Whatever you're about to say, whether it's that I'm beginning to believe Grammy's nonsense, or I'm falling for you, or I'm trying to figure out how to stay in Wagon Train, none of that. I'm not!"

He set his unfinished drink on the bedside table and shifted to face her. Taking her drink from her hand, he reached behind him and put it on the table, too. Then he cradled her face in his big hands. "You may not be, but I am."

"W-what do you m-mean?" If only she could stop shaking.

"I mean, crazy as it sounds since we only met two days ago, I crave you more than any woman I've ever known."

"You m-mean for s-sex?"

"Not just that. Our sex is amazing, but the connection is deeper."

"B-because it's C-christmas?"

"No! It's *you.* You fit, *we* fit, and it scares the hell out of me, because it's not… I know what I want, and—"

"I'm not it." Her shakes disappeared, leaving her with a heavy heart. For him. For her. "You're falling for the wrong person."

"Yes."

"Me, too." She gazed into his beautiful stormy eyes. "What are we going to do?"

He sucked in a breath. "I could take you home now. We could cut it off clean instead of putting ourselves through this."

"We have the fair. The video."

"Maybe we could get through that with a minimum of—"

"I don't want the minimum. I want the maximum."

His eyes darkened. "Even if we make things worse for ourselves?"

"Yes, but you have a vote, too. If you'd rather stop now, then we will."

"I don't want to stop."

"Then make love to me, Bret. Make love to me until dawn."

23

Moving carefully so he wouldn't wake Molly, Bret rolled over, picked up his phone from the nightstand and shut off the alarm before it chimed. She'd conked out an hour ago, but he hadn't been able to sleep.

They hadn't made love until dawn, but they'd come doggone close. He wished he could let her sleep, but they'd promised her grandmother they'd be back before Zach woke up.

She could have a few more minutes, though. He'd spent the past hour going over their situation. And going over it again. He couldn't possibly be in love, could he? He'd rejected her suggestion that Christmas had affected his thinking. He refused to believe he was the kind of sap who'd make the same mistake two years in a row.

It wasn't Christmas messing with his mind. Yeah, they'd met at a Christmas tree lot. They'd cruised down Main Street with carols on the radio and they'd made love after he'd spent a couple of hours creating holiday luminarias for a client's

Christmas display. Tonight they'd decorated her grandmother's tree together.

But this wasn't a replay of last year. Molly wasn't anything like Jennifer. Molly wasn't like any woman he'd ever dated. Of course she wasn't. He'd never dated a woman who had a child. Wouldn't have knowingly chosen to do that.

If she'd been up front with him from the start, she wouldn't be in his bed now. And he would have missed so much. She made his cock ache with longing, but she made his heart ache, too.

He had crazy thoughts about saying to hell with his misgivings and asking her to marry him. Marry him! After knowing her less than two full days!

And what if he did such a stupid thing? She'd have to reject him because she wouldn't be willing to live the rest of her days in a town with no job opportunities for someone with her background.

But that didn't matter because he wasn't going to commit emotional suicide by going against his own logic and good judgment. Marrying a woman who already had one kid and wanted another one ASAP was the exact opposite of the direction he'd settled on.

Oh, and having these thoughts after knowing her less than forty-eight hours? If Gil found out, he'd likely lock him in his house for the rest of the holiday. With the support of the entire family.

"What time is it?" Her voice had a velvety texture.

His cock liked the sound of it way too much. "You're awake?"

"No, I talk in my sleep. About time. I'm always asking about the time."

"Smartass." He rolled to his side, facing her.

"You didn't sleep, did you?"

"How do you know?"

"I didn't hear any snoring."

"I don't snore. But you do. Like a freight train."

"No, I don't." She punched him lightly on the shoulder.

"No, you don't." He gathered her close. Couldn't stop himself. "You made a few cute little snuffling sounds, but no snoring."

She snuggled close. "Why didn't you sleep? You had to be exhausted."

"I should be. Instead I'm wired. Shouldn't have had the coffee with the sugar cookies. Bad combo."

"Does coffee keep you up?"

"Oh, yeah." He cupped her delicious bottom. "You probably noticed. I was up a *lot*."

"Including now."

"Yes, ma'am, but we're not doing anything about it." He gave her a quick kiss, let her go and climbed out of bed. "We need to be out the door in fifteen minutes if we're gonna keep our promise to your grandmother."

"And we're keeping that promise." She threw back the covers. "Brrr."

"I'll go turn up the heat." He walked out of the bedroom, away from temptation. He couldn't see her beautiful body clearly, but he didn't need to. He breathed in the aroma of arousal, his and hers. He could still taste her on his tongue.

After goosing up the heat, he stood in the hall and pictured little Zach asleep in his crib, unaware that his mommy was miles away. Causing that baby any distress whatsoever was not part of this deal.

Molly had turned on the bedside lamp but fortunately she was mostly dressed when he walked back in. She tucked her shirt into her jeans. "Do you happen to have a spare toothbrush?"

"No, but you can borrow mine."

"You wouldn't be grossed out?"

"I've spent most of the night with my tongue in your mouth. I think I can handle sharing a toothbrush." He took clean underwear out of a drawer. He wasn't going to dig in the hamper. Not in front of Molly.

She laughed. "Good point. It's just that some people—"

"I'm not some people." He tugged on his briefs and sat on the bed so he could put on his socks.

"No, you're certainly not." She headed for the bathroom.

Would she close the door? She did not. Evidently she felt as comfortable with him as he felt with her. Maybe her grammy was right about the compatibility factor. She knew her granddaughter and she knew him. With Mrs. J, who needed a dating app?

Except she hadn't known everything about him. If she had, she might not have tried to play Cupid.

Molly came out of the bathroom with her hair brushed and probably her teeth, too. No makeup. He liked the fact she hadn't felt the need to put any on.

She smiled. "The toothbrush is all yours. Good choice, by the way. The bristles are just right—not too soft and not too firm."

"Glad you approve. I'll just be a minute. I'm not going to bother to shave."

"Good. You look sexy with a little scruff."

"And you look sexy just by existing."

"I know." She gave a little shimmy. "It's my superpower."

He stood there, stunned and speechless. Dear God, he loved her. He. Loved. Molly. Now what?

"Bret? Are you okay? You just went all deer in the headlights."

He snapped out of it. "Yep!" *Excuse! Find one! Fast!* "I just had the horrible thought that I might be low on gas. I've been preoccupied and I can't remember the last time I filled up."

"Yikes. Like we might not make it back to town?"

"No, no. I'm sure we will. But I need to fill up before I come back out here." He made tracks for the bathroom. Whew. He'd have to be on guard from now on. No telling what he might blurt out in a weak moment.

He splashed cold water on his face. That helped. Probably needed a good hard slap, too. Gil would be happy to accommodate him, but then he'd have to admit why he needed it. Nobody could know about this. Nobody.

Picking up the toothbrush, he put a little paste on the bristles. She liked his toothbrush. He'd never enjoyed using it more than he did this morning. He was in love. Heaven help him.

Before they left, he turned off all the lights.

She hurried down the steps and started around to the passenger side. "Do you do that whenever you leave?"

"Do what?"

"Turn off all the lights."

"Yes, ma'am." He helped her in.

"Then Gil must have turned them on for you when he came over to set up the condom tree."

"Damn. I forgot to dismantle it so I could give the condoms back to Rance." He closed the door, jogged around to the driver's side and climbed in.

"Is it urgent to get them back today? Does he have a hot date tonight?"

"Well, if he does, he'll have to fetch them from my house himself." He closed the door and buckled up. "If he has any sense, he kept some in reserve." He switched on the engine.

"I really think he's making a mistake with those decorated packages. It's one thing if a woman gives them to a guy as a cute joke, but for a guy to show up with them... I doubt he'll get the response he's hoping for."

"Who knows? Maybe by using them, he'll find the perfect partner, someone who appreciates his unique sense of humor."

"I suppose that's possible, too." She leaned over and peered at the dash. "You have three-quarters of a tank."

"I do? Huh. I must have filled it up on autopilot." He'd stopped for gas Wednesday morning on the way into the shop, something he routinely did whenever snow was predicted. She didn't have to know that.

Except she might suspect something. She kept looking at him like he was a bug under a microscope. Might as well ask. "What's up?"

"I haven't known you long, but I don't peg you as the kind of guy who fails to monitor his gas tank, especially in the winter, when running out can have serious consequences."

"I knew I had enough gas."

"So what made you go all googly-eyed?"

"You. That cute little shimmy almost made me grab you and toss you onto the bed."

"You could have said that."

"Talking about it would have stirred me up even more. I had to get control of myself. Focusing on gas tank issues helped."

"You're that susceptible?"

"Seems like I am."

"Then I'll watch myself. I don't want to cause you—"

"Aw, no, Molly. Please don't go all self-conscious on me. That would be a crime. Do your thing. Don't worry about how it will affect me."

"Okay." She was quiet for a bit. "It is startling how we've come so far so fast."

"Tell me about it."

"Is this *anything* like your last Christmas situation? Because that does worry me."

"It's nothing like it. That period in my life was like living inside a vat of pink cotton candy."

"Yuck!"

"Exactly."

"What's this like?"

"Living inside a vat of warm dark chocolate."

"Oooo."

"Yeah, I know." He glanced over at her. "You get to me, Miss Molly, but I can handle it. I'll work on the googly-eye part. I can tell it freaked you out."

"I thought you were having a fit."

"I was, sort of. I know what. If I act like that again, especially if we're with other people, ask me when I last filled up the gas tank. That'll snap me out of it."

She grinned. "It'll be our catch phrase."

"Yes, ma'am." Good, they were joking about it. It wasn't a joking matter, but he'd keep that info to himself.

24

Bret dropped Molly off with a sweet goodbye kiss, but he didn't linger. She wasn't surprised to find her grandmother up despite the early hour. As she slowly opened the front door to keep the bells from jingling, Grammy walked into the foyer.

"I took the bells off," she murmured. "Zach's still asleep. Ditch your things and come into the kitchen. I made oatmeal."

"Yum." And coffee. She could smell it. Did Bret like oatmeal? She'd bet he did. A sensual treat for a sensual guy.

She walked into the cozy kitchen with its color scheme of yellow, blue and white. A person could not be depressed in this kitchen even if they tried.

Grammy had dished them each a bowl with a pat of butter in the middle, exactly as her mother had served it when Molly had lived at home. Raisins, brown sugar, and cream sat on the table to be added according to each person's preference. Molly loved it all.

"This hits the spot. Thank you." She took the mug of coffee her grandmother handed her and sat.

"I was hoping Zach would sleep in a bit so we'd have a chance to talk."

"He should. He was up later than usual." Molly doctored her oatmeal with all the goodies, popped a spoonful into her mouth and hummed with pleasure. She'd loved this combination of flavors since she'd been a toddler.

She took another bite, and another. "This is fabulous. Thank you."

"I've been eating it for seventy-plus years, and I still love it."

"Mom's tastes exactly the same. Can you believe I stopped making it when I was married?"

"Aaron didn't like it?"

"Hated oatmeal. Even the smell of it, so I gave it up. I made some last winter, but it didn't taste this good. I thought I didn't like it anymore, but I'll watch how you do it next time."

"I have a couple of tricks I'll show you." She picked up her coffee mug. "Can I ask how it went?"

"You sure can." She met her kind gaze. "We had a wonderful time. Thank you. Bret asked me to thank you, too."

"That sounds like him. You're both welcome."

"I found out something, though. Something important. He's dead set against bringing kids into a relationship until the couple has a chance to get to know each other." She glanced at her grandmother. "I'll bet you didn't know that."

Her eyelashes fluttered. "Actually, I—"

"You knew?"

"He told me the morning after he stayed the night here."

"Why didn't you tell me?"

"It wasn't mine to tell. He confided in me, and it was clear he wasn't planning to bring it up since he was convinced you two had no future."

"Do you know why he feels that way?"

"Yes."

"You're not going to tell me, are you?"

"No, honey, I'm not. That's up to him. But I'm curious as to why he mentioned this to you, since nothing's changed. You're still expecting to get a job somewhere else. You sent out all those resumes, and you will get hired. I have no doubt."

That prospect didn't excite her anymore. "Well, supposedly he told me for my sake. He sensed I was falling for him."

"Hmm."

"But when I said that wasn't true, he admitted he was falling for me."

"I knew it!" She clapped a hand over her mouth and glanced upward as if expecting to hear Zach. Silence.

"But he doesn't want to fall for me, Grammy."

"I understand that, but—"

"I'm the wrong person for him. I'll be relocating and I already have a kid.

She waved a hand. "Details."

"Significant details." She kept her voice down. Hashing this out with her grandmother was important and if Zach woke up, they wouldn't get to. "We considered breaking up."

"Breaking up? After two nights? Oh, well, I suppose that's how it is these days. Everything happening at top speed, nobody taking time to—"

"We decided not to."

"Oh. Well, good. Then there's hope."

"Not really. But we can't stand the idea of ending things when we'll still be in the same town, running into each other at the bank, the grocery store. Especially since I've abandoned the idea of keeping Zach a secret."

"Really?" Grammy's eyebrows lifted. "That's news."

"It wasn't a great plan in the first place. Bret's right that I have very little chance of finding a man mature enough to be a good dad to Zach and who's also fine with moving away."

"Not impossible, though. It was worth a shot."

"And we gave it one. Dragging it out any longer isn't fair to Zach. He needs to meet more people than you, me, Bret and the pizza boy. Which reminds me, would you like to go out to the ranch for a sleighride on Sunday?"

"They have a sleigh out there?"

"Just bought it."

"I'd love it. Zach would, too. And by the way, since you haven't broken up with Bret, I'll watch him—"

"He's busy. Tomorrow night, too."

"Oh?"

"Bret and Gil have a routine they follow on Friday and Saturday nights during a fair. They stay in town, which makes it easier to coordinate what they need to do with the booth."

"Makes sense." How's the video coming along?"

"Good. Now that I have those six luminarias to work with and the things I picked up in Missoula yesterday, I can add the finishing touches with shots of the lanterns glowing and a wintery scene outside, maybe with a few snowflakes falling if I'm lucky."

"Let me know if you need help minding Zach while you do that."

"I'll try to do it while he naps." She yawned.

Grammy smiled, her expression indulgent. "You look like you could use one."

"I'll be fine."

"Probably, since you have fifty years on me. There was a time I could stay up all night making love and still function the next day. But those times are gone."

"We didn't stay up *all*—"

"Molly."

"Okay we did. Mostly. I got about an hour's sleep. I don't think he slept at all."

"And he'll be welding today?"

She gasped. "Yes! Oh, my Lord, what if he hurts himself? That torch is dangerous. If he burns himself because of me, I'll never—"

"He's a grown man. Trust him to know his limits."

"I do, but—"

"He'll be fine. Gil's working with him. They watch out for each other."

"They do, but...hang on. I have to show you something." She quickly left the table and came back with her phone. "You'll laugh when you see this, so if you don't want to wake up Zach... be prepared."

"I'm ready." She put on her glasses.

Picking the best picture of the condom tree, she handed over her phone.

Grammy peered at it, then enlarged the image. Grabbing a napkin, she used it to muffle her giggles.

Molly took back the phone and scrolled to the closeups she'd taken of each holiday image, showing them one by one. Then she laid her phone down. "Gil's handiwork."

"Those boys." Grammy cleared her throat and took off her glasses so she could wipe her eyes. "That's hysterical. Did you use those?"

"That's the kicker. Gil had the idea but Rance had the condoms and he wants them all back."

"He wants them returned? What a doofus."

"Every last one."

"Oh, for heaven's sake. He couldn't have spared a few? I trust you had backup."

"We did."

"I'm not surprised Rance thinks holiday-themed condoms are the ticket, though. He's been full of mischief from the get-go."

"I asked Bret if I could be there when he gives them back, but that might not work out. We never got around to taking them off the tree."

"I wonder why you never got around to that chore?"

Her cheeks grew warm.

"I'm teasing because I'm so happy you had a lovely time. I wish you could take a nap this morning, but knowing you, that won't happen until that video's done."

"It shouldn't take me that long. Then I'll drive over to the shop so they can give it a test run. Bret's going to see if he can get one of his brothers to bag up the condoms and bring them to town. If that happens, I'll time my visit to coincide with returning them to Rance."

"That should be worth the price of admission. When are you going to the fair?"

"In the morning. Now that Zach's no longer a secret, I thought I'd take him. Want to come with us?"

She hesitated, then gave a quick nod. "Yes. Yes, I do. I used to go all the time."

"With Grandpa, I'll bet." She reached over and squeezed Grammy's arm.

"He loved it. So did I. The whole town turns out."

"The whole town?"

"Pretty much. The Christmas fair is special. They have carolers, food booths, and... oh, my goodness, I forgot about this. Santa will be there!"

"You mean walking around going *ho, ho, ho*?"

"I mean sitting on an elaborate throne-type thing so the kids can tell him what they want for Christmas. Desiree McLintock's bookstore sponsors it, the Wenches dress up as elves to shepherd the kids in and out, and Santa is our own Andy Hartmann, editor of the *Sentinel.* We have to get a picture of Zach with Santa."

"Bret told me the same thing, but he didn't say it was part of the fair."

"*Bret* suggested taking Zach to see Santa?"

"He did." She'd been so touched by his offer to help with Zach's album that she hadn't asked for details about the Santa visit. "It seems silly to me since Zach's so young, but Bret thinks it's important."

"Which it is. Props to that boy. I have a cute outfit for Zach that I found at the Baby Barn. I was going to give it to him on Christmas Eve so he could wear it Christmas Day, but this is better. I'll bust it out early."

"Let me guess. It's an elf outfit."

"How did you know?"

"Beau and Jess bought one for Maverick for her Santa picture."

"Listen to you, spouting off info about Bret's family."

"I have to admit the McLintocks sound like fun."

"Especially the sixth son?"

She sighed in resignation. "Yes, Grammy, especially him. You win. You said I'd like him and I do."

"But you're not falling for him. That's what you said, right?"

"That's what I told him."

"Hmm."

"I think I hear Zach." Picking up her dishes, she quickly rinsed them and put them in the dishwasher. She clattered around, not worried about waking Zach anymore.

Grammy had a way of worming the truth out of her. Time to end this cozy little chat.

25

Bret glanced at the clock. “Molly will be here in about ten minutes. Ready to call it quits?”

“I’m almost done with this one.” Gil continued to work. “I’m impressed with the number we managed to produce, bro.”

“Me, too. If they all sell, that’ll at least pay for our booth.”

“Which’ll be good. We don’t know if Christmas shoppers will be ordering gates and such.”

“Guess we’ll find out.” He put the final touches on his last luminaria. “I’m shutting down.”

“I’ll be right behind you. I’m curious to see this video. Find out if you’ve got star power.”

“She says I do.”

“Yeah, well, wait until she gets a look at my handsome mug. She’ll be itching to take a new video.”

“You know what? She suggested we put out a welding tutorial. And a blacksmithing one, for that matter. I’d be lousy at that, but you could do it with your hands tied behind your back.”

"And hold the torch with my teeth?" He doused the flame and began closing valves. "Hey, I wonder if that's possible. I could get on talk shows with that trick. I could—"

"Sorry I brought it up." He moved the luminaria out of Rivet's reach. She'd be happy to see Molly again, but not as happy as he'd be.

"Seriously, the tutorial's a good idea. I admit this woman sounds interesting. I can't wait to see Rance's face when she personally hands over the sack of condoms."

"She's not shy." He hung up his apron and goggles. Ran his fingers through his hair. Tucked his shirt in a little better.

"Clearly, or she wouldn't have timed this visit to coincide with the condom bag exchange." Gil looked out the window. "An itty bitty sedan just pulled up."

His heart began to race. "That'll be her."

"Is that the car she planned to use to haul a ten-foot spruce? Maybe she's not so smart, after all."

"She's smart enough, but she also enjoys a challenge."

"No wonder she likes you, then." He grinned. "You've always been a challenge."

"Nice, bro. I love you, too."

"Go greet her. I'll let Rivet out and turn on the laptop."

"Thanks." He barely registered what Gil said. He was already headed for the door with Molly on the brain. Maybe he should go out and help her with — what? She was only bringing a thumb drive. She could probably manage that without assistance.

He was a mess. A lovesick, needy mess. He wouldn't get to hold her tonight. Or tomorrow night. He should have rented a room at the hotel. Why hadn't he worked it out so that—

She was almost at the door. He opened it. "Hi."

Her smile filled his vision. "Hi, yourself."

"I've missed you."

"Missed you, too." Standing on tiptoe, she put a gloved hand on his chest and give him a quick kiss on the mouth. "Can I come in?"

"Oh." He stepped back to give her room. "Absolutely." His lips tingled. Maybe he could grab another quick kiss before his brother—

"You must be Gil." She laughed. "Creator of condom trees."

Too late.

"Yes, ma'am. You're a good sport."

"It was clever. And here comes Rivet!" She glanced over her shoulder. "Better close the door, Bret."

Oh, yeah. The door. He shut out the cold air sweeping into the room and turned around. Molly had taken off her gloves and crouched down to pet Rivet.

Gil stood gazing at him with a knowing expression.

He shrugged. And smiled.

Gil mouthed *pathetic* and shook his head.

Standing, Molly unbuttoned her trench coat. "We should get going. I want to finish showing you this before Cheyenne arrives with the condoms. I don't want anyone to see it but you guys."

Gil looked confused. "Why?"

"Because we'll lose the element of surprise. It's more fun if nobody else has seen it, including members of your family." She slid her arms out of her coat sleeves.

And he belatedly remembered his manners. "Let me hang that up for you."

"Thanks." She handed it over with another one of those smiles that had become like water in the desert. Then she turned back to Gil. "At least that's my thought. But if you want to show it to Cheyenne, and Rance, too, when he arrives, that's up to you, of course."

"I vote we go with your plan." Gil glanced at him. "Okay with you, Bret?" His subtle smirk said he knew damn well it was.

"Fine with me."

Molly took a thumb drive from the pocket of her jeans. "Let's load 'er up."

"Laptop's on a little table in the back," Gil said. "Screen's on the wall. Is it big enough for what you have in mind?" He led the way, followed by Molly, who was followed by Rivet, the tip of her tail curved, a question mark.

Bret was in no hurry. Now that he was about to see himself on the screen, he was nervous. He'd done some show-offy moves that night to impress her. What if he looked like a dork?

"The screen size is fine." Molly sounded so calm. Evidently not going bananas like he was.

"Grammy filled me in on the scope of the fair and the emphasis on Christmas. You don't want a ginormous screen that takes away from Santa and the carolers."

"Are you bringing Zach in the morning?" He'd blurted it out, although it had nothing to do with the matter at hand. He just wanted to know.

She looked over her shoulder. "I am. Grammy approves of your idea of a picture with Santa. She even has an elf outfit for him she picked up at the Baby Barn."

"Are you bringing your camcorder?" He'd already skipped ahead to the next time he'd see her because this visit would be short.

"I hadn't planned on it, but—"

"If Gil can spare me from the booth, I'll help you. Like with carrying stuff. Or carrying Zach."

"I can spare you." Gil sounded like he was two seconds from cracking up. He opened the laptop. "Got that thumb drive, Molly?"

"Right here." She handed it to him and seconds later, the video was loaded, ready to play. The title page said *MCLINTOCK METALWORKS, Bringing the Heat.*

Gil chuckled. "Catchy. I like it." He hit Play.

And Bret was face-to-face with himself, working to background music that sounded vaguely like Mannheim Steamroller. His breath caught. He'd been in photos a million times, even in videos from family events.

This was different. Either Molly had a gift for making him look like a stud, or, less likely, he did look like one.

"Wow." Gil stared at the screen. "I hate to say it, bro, but you look good. Molly, is that background music Mannheim Steamroller?"

"That would cost too much in royalty fees. I found some free stuff that sounds something like them."

Gil nodded. "Nicely done. Oh, hey, the luminarias sure are effective, lit up like that."

"Sure are." Bret studied the flickering lights set in a darkened window with snow falling outside. "When did you take this part? You couldn't have done it today."

"Yes, I did. We had a few flurries mid-morning. Very lucky."

"But it looks dark out there."

"I found the technique online. I had to make a quick trip to Missoula yesterday for something called neutral density filters. You put them over the window, underexpose the shot, and it looks like nighttime. Neat, huh?"

"Very much so." The video ended with a closeup of his sweat-covered face, the glow from the torch highlighting his cheekbones and the firm set of his mouth. He looked dedicated to the task. And manly, if he did say so himself. The last screen was labeled with the company name, the phone number and the website url.

Gil let out a low whistle. "Nice job, Molly."

"Thank you." She turned around. "Bret? Did you like it?"

"Yes, ma'am." If Gil would just magically disappear, he could kiss her. "It's wonderful."

"Very well done." Gil checked the time on the laptop. "I'd like to watch it again, but we'd better not. Cheyenne isn't due for a little while, but he could show up early." He glanced at Molly. "How long have you been doing this?"

"Not long. It's fun for me. I had to talk your brother into the idea."

"I'm glad you did. I predict it'll be a crowd-pleaser this weekend, and the luminarias we've stockpiled will go fast." He ejected the thumb drive and turned off the laptop. "Now I'm feeling guilty about the condom tree."

Bret ducked his head so Gil wouldn't catch his smile.

"Oh, don't feel guilty." Molly took out her phone. "It makes a great story. I took pictures. Showed them to Grammy this morning." She turned her phone so Gil could see and scrolled through them.

"You showed these to Mrs. J?" Now he looked really uncomfortable. Served him right.

"She got a laugh out of it."

"Uh, good, I guess. And here comes Cheyenne. With Kendall. Didn't know she was planning to be here."

The shop door opened and Kendall stormed in followed by Cheyenne carrying the bag of condoms. "Gil McLintock, you should be ashamed of yourself." The top of her head barely reached the shoulder of any man in the room, but she was so full of energy it didn't matter that she wasn't tall. Bret admired the heck out of her.

She hurried toward Molly, hand outstretched. "Hi, I'm Kendall. I'd love to tell you that the rest of the McLintock gang isn't as nutty as Gil and Rance, but I'd be lying. I love them all to pieces, but we have some doozies in this family."

He couldn't let that stand. "Hey, c'mon, Kendall. I invited her out to the ranch on Sunday for a sleigh ride, so don't go giving us a bad rep before she even gets there."

"Don't blame me, Bret. I'm not the one who put a condom tree right inside your front door last night. Molly, I hope you weren't too upset."

"Apparently she wasn't," Gil said. "She took pictures and showed them to Mrs. J this morning."

Kendall looked at Molly, her eyes gleaming with approval. "Excellent! Too bad Mrs. J's not the librarian anymore. She could cancel their library cards."

Molly laughed. "I don't think she would if she could. She thought it was funny. So did I."

"Well, it's a good thing you ladies have a sense of humor. I was ready to smack somebody." She gave Gil the evil eye.

The door opened again and Rance strutted in. "Hey, is this a party? If I'd known, I could've brought..." He trailed off. "Oh." He gazed at Molly and color rose from the collar of his sheepskin jacket. "I reckon you're Miss Molly." He took off his hat.

"And I reckon you're Rance." She came forward, pausing to take the bag from Cheyenne before walking up to their baby brother. "They're all here, but you can take them out and count them if you want."

His color deepened. "No ma'am. That won't be necessary. And I would just like to say—"

"First let me say something. These are kind of cute, in a nerdy sort of way."

He winced.

"But take my advice. Don't say a word to your date about these in advance. She'll likely run like the wind."

"Why?"

"Because they're only funny if you say nothing and just let her see them after she's all hot and bothered. Then she might laugh and you'll get points for being clever. But if you flash them around prematurely, she's liable to think you're just dopey. You could ruin your chances."

"Yes, ma'am. Thank you, ma'am."

"Here you go." She handed him the bag.

"Thank you, ma'am. Much obliged. I'd better get back to work. See you all later." Cramming his hat on, he started out the door. Then he turned back. "Nice meetin' you, ma'am!" Then he was gone.

"I love it!" Kendall exchanged a high five with Molly. "Bret, this one's a keeper."

And that was the tragedy of it. He nodded. "Yes, she is."

26

Grammy offered to drive her Subaru to the high school gym the next morning and Molly accepted with gratitude. Packing a bag with her camera equipment was easy. Organizing a bag for Zach that would cover all contingencies was complicated. She hadn't taken him for an outing in more than a month and she'd forgotten what a production it was.

Besides diapers, wipes, bottles, bibs and baby food, she had to figure out how to keep him warm and yet dressed in the elf outfit. She ended up putting him in a sleeper and adding the elf outfit on top of it. Luckily, the outfit was big on him.

At the last minute, Grammy hauled out another gift she'd planned to put under the tree — a fold-up wagon. Molly gave her grandmother the biggest hug ever. The problem of lugging her child, his paraphernalia and her camera equipment was solved.

"We used to have wooden red wagons," Grammy said as she drove to the high school with Zach ensconced in his car seat in the back. "Or metal. These canvas fold-up ones are brilliant. Same concept and they're portable."

"It's perfect. I can't imagine a better gift." She glanced over at her grandmother. "I hope you don't have much more tucked away. You've already given me the video camera and the wagon."

"The wagon's for Zach."

"You also bought the elf outfit, which is adorable, by the way."

"Also for Zach."

"No, it isn't. Bret says the picture with Santa isn't for the kid. Oh, maybe when he or she is older they'll get a kick out of it. But it's mostly for the parents and grandparents."

"Bret is correct. I told you he was raised right. I'm surprised your mother hasn't asked whether you're planning to get a picture of Zach with Santa."

"She's distracted, worried about Grandma Irene."

"Yep. I called her yesterday while you were delivering the video. She hates missing Zach's first Christmas."

"I'll call her, maybe this afternoon. This week just got away from me."

"She knows you're busy."

"Did you tell her about Bret?"

"No. It wasn't my—"

"Wasn't your story to tell. You're good about that, Grammy. And truthfully, I don't know if it's wise to say anything."

"Might be better not to. She has a lot on her plate."

"I won't mention it." That was a relief. She didn't want to discuss Bret with her mom. Not yet, anyway. "Look at that. We're here already."

"You're always *here already* in Wagon Train."

That made her laugh. "What should we head for first? Santa?"

"Are you for real? We'll start with McLintock Metalworks to see that video in operation."

She grinned. "Okay."

"You know you want to. I can't imagine why you'd suggest anything else." She pulled into a parking space, one of the few left in the crowded lot.

"I was thinking of the elf outfit when I suggested Santa first. So far Zach hasn't drooled on it or spit up on it. That could change any minute."

"Then we'll stop at the Metalworks booth, check out the video setup and whether sales are good, then we'll snag Bret and go over to see Santa. You know he wants to be there."

"I'm sure he does. He even offered to carry stuff for me, but this wagon is a better option." She opened the passenger door and started to get out.

"Well, dammit."

"What?" She swung back around. "Is something wrong?"

"It never occurred to me that giving you that wagon would take away Bret's excuse to use his manly muscles."

"You're funny."

"We could leave the wagon in the car."

"Nuh-uh. I love that wagon. Zach will love riding in it. It'll be a great place to put our coats once we're inside. Anyway, Bret doesn't need that kind of validation."

Grammy sighed. "In my day, we would have left the wagon in the car."

"In my day, we don't fake helplessness so a man can feel worthy."

Her grandmother gazed at her and nodded. "You're so right. Forgive my retro thinking. Let's go get the wagon."

"Let's do."

The asphalt lot had been cleared of snow, so Grammy unfolded the wagon next to the back passenger door. Zach went in first with a blanket tucked around him for warmth. Then they added his bag of supplies. The camera bag fit exactly in the space left.

Molly stood back. "It's like we planned it this way. He's wedged in so tight he's not going anywhere."

"I'm taking a picture. All we need is some plastic reindeer and he'd look like he's appropriated Santa's job."

"He does! Whatcha think, baby boy? Ready to go for a ride?"

Zach grinned, showing off his one bottom tooth.

"Then off we go." She grabbed the metal handle and pulled the wagon and her giggling child across the lot and through the double doors into the cheerful chaos of the Wagon Train Christmas Fair.

Zach's eyes widened and his little rosebud mouth made a perfect circle as he took in his surroundings. She pulled the blanket off so he wouldn't overheat. The gym was cool, though, so the extra layer under the elf outfit had been a wise move.

Thank goodness she'd chosen to break him out of isolation so he could experience this event.

So much color, dominated by red, green, silver and gold. So many holiday aromas — cinnamon, peppermint and fresh evergreen. The pine scent came from the booth opposite the entrance, which had wreaths and garlands for sale.

As Molly took off her coat, she surveyed the area. "Is there a map posted somewhere?"

"Never has been. The vendors have one but not the shoppers. I think that's on purpose. You buy more if you wander around aimlessly." She cocked her head. "Hear the carolers?"

Molly paused. Voices harmonizing to the melody of *Greensleeves* penetrated the din of conversation and laughter. She glanced down at Zach. Wonder shone in his dark eyes and the Christmas spirit spilled over her like... rivulets of maple syrup. "I already love this fair."

Her grandmother smiled. "It's awesome, isn't it? Zach's mesmerized."

"Yep. He loves it."

"Will our coats block his view?"

"Not if we mash them down a bit. There we go. He can still see."

"Let's keep going down this aisle. My instincts tell me McLintock Metalworks is—"

"Oh, it's Mrs. J! Marsh, Mrs. J is here!" A tall blonde came hurrying toward them.

"Ella Bradley!" Grammy beamed at her and squeezed her outstretched hands. "It's so good to see you. This is my—"

"Your granddaughter. Word has gotten around." She held out her hand to Molly. "I'm so glad to meet you. This is my fiancé, Marsh McLintock."

The broad-shouldered cowboy by her side tipped his hat and smiled. "It's a pleasure, Molly. Good job putting my little brother Rance in his place yesterday. Gil's a bit remorseful, too. Does my heart good."

"Bret was kind of upset, but I really wasn't. That said, I couldn't resist a chance to personally return Rance's stash, since he had the nerve to ask for it back."

"Wish I'd been there." He tipped his hat in her grandmother's direction. "Mrs. J. Always great to see you."

"Same here, Marsh. Looks like congratulations are in order. I always wondered if you and Ella would end up together."

"Took more than twenty years for me to finally convince her."

"Yeah." Ella chuckled. "I can be pretty dense."

"Well, evidently it was worth the wait. You're both glowing. Hey, we're on our way to check out the Metalworks booth. Where is it?"

"We'll lead you to it," Marsh said. "We just came from there. Just follow us and we'll—"

"Hang on a sec, Marsh." Ella caught his arm. "I didn't get to meet this little guy." She crouched down and made eye contact with Zach. "What's your name, cutie-pie?"

"Sorry about that," Molly said. "He's Zach, my son."

Ella smiled at him. "Zach, you're adorable. You look just like your mom."

He studied her, as if sizing her up.

"What do you think of all this, kiddo? Amazing, huh?"

He stared at her for another couple of seconds. Then he sucked in a breath and launched into his baby-speak, babbling away non-stop until he ran out of air.

"Oh, my God, too cute for words." Ella grinned. "Zach, I can't wait to see how you turn out." She stood and glanced at Marsh. "Lead on. I'll walk with Molly so we can exchange numbers."

"Got it. Come with me, Mrs. J."

Ella fell into step beside Molly and pulled out her phone. "Give me your number and I'll text you mine. Then if you need to change him while you're here, text me and I'll let you into the girls' locker room. It's better than the restroom."

"That's very kind." She rattled off her number. "Do you work here?"

"I'm a PE teacher." Ella tapped on her phone. "There you go. All set." She tucked her phone away. "Zach's just soaking this up, isn't he?"

"He absolutely is. I'm so glad I brought him."

"I've been coming to this ever since I was old enough to sit on Santa's lap."

"I gathered you grew up here since you've known Marsh for so long."

"Sure did. We've been best friends since kindergarten, but I never dreamed we'd end up engaged. Life is full of surprises."

"I met Kendall yesterday and found out she's lived on a neighboring ranch since she was little."

"Yep. Had a huge crush on Cheyenne for years. Finally made him see the light."

"Did Beau and Jess grow up together, too?"

"In a way. They were in the same class but I don't think they had much to do with each other until she moved back to help her dad with the *Sentinel.*"

"Hometown girl, though."

"True. I guess there's sort of a pattern, although Sky's wife Penny is from California."

"That's still three out of four." No wonder Bret felt the way he did. His brothers had all chosen someone born and raised here.

"I heard you aren't planning to stay in Wagon Train, something about the job market?"

She sighed. "The job possibilities are slim to none. Maybe it's just as well."

"Or maybe you need to think outside the box."

"You sound like Grammy."

"I hope so. Mrs. J's one of my idols." She took a breath. "Okay, I'll go out on a limb, here. I watched your video, and Molly, you captured the essence of Bret McLintock. It's like you've known him forever. And I'm qualified to say that because I *have* known him forever. You nailed it."

"Sometimes it feels as if we... I dunno... met in another life or something. Now *I'm* sounding like Grammy."

"If I were you, I'd trust that feeling. If there's any way you guys can work this out..."

"I don't think there is." Glancing down the aisle, she zeroed in on him standing near the McLintock Metalworks booth, scanning the crowd. Her chest warmed and her stomach fluttered.

He spotted her and smiled.

She smiled back. Joy flooded through her, stronger and richer than the Christmas spirit. Quite likely she'd have to give him up someday. This wasn't that day.

27

Bret curbed his first impulse and didn't maneuver his way through the crowd so he'd get to Molly sooner. He stayed put and let her come to him. Gil had lectured him about his unseemly eagerness. His worshipful stare.

In an outright lie, he'd sworn he wasn't in love with her, that he couldn't possibly be in love after such a short time. Gil hadn't believed a word of it.

Soon his entire family would discover the embarrassing truth that he'd fallen in love in the space of three days. They'd lived with him way too long to be fooled by his lame protestations and his stumbling rationalizations. Cheyenne and Kendall already had the goods on him. Rance would have picked up on the situation, too, except he'd run out of the shop like his hair was on fire.

Shifting restlessly, he waited for Molly, who was pulling a wagon. That meant she wouldn't need him to lug anything, but as a bonus, he'd have his hands free. Or one, at least. He'd use the other to pull the wagon with Zach sitting in it, cute as hell in his green elf suit.

What a kid. He was getting bouncy in that wagon and Bret wanted to believe the munchkin was excited because he'd spotted his spit-fest partner.

Mrs. J looked happy to see him, too. That soothed his nerves since he hadn't faced her since having hours of hot sex with her granddaughter. Molly had insisted Mrs. J's flower-child history would help in that department, but he hadn't been fully convinced.

Yes, Molly was an adult in charge of her life, but Mrs. J was protective. Any fool could see that. If he trampled on Molly's feelings, he'd answer to Mrs. J. That meant he had to give Molly a better explanation for his position than he'd supplied so far. The sooner, the better.

Marsh and Mrs. J led the parade, so she was the first one to greet him. "Hi, there, Bret."

"Good morning, Mrs. J. How's the fair been so far?"

"It all looks fascinating, but truthfully, this is the first booth I've given any real attention to." She waved her hand at him. "Could you please step to your left so I can see that video Molly made?"

"You haven't seen it?" He glanced at Molly and lifted his eyebrows.

"I didn't show it to her. You were the client. I wanted you and Gil to be the first to view it."

Mrs. J was close enough to give him a nudge. "Obviously she has professional ethics. Now move aside so I can see."

He gave her room. "It's on a loop. This is the end, so if you wait, you'll—"

"Hush, Bret. This is the good part. Oh, Molly, you captured his artistic dedication right there! Sweat glistening on his face, his jaw tight. Bravo!"

"Thank you, Grammy."

He looked past Mrs. J and into Molly's dark eyes. His happy place. "People love your video."

"I'm glad, but is it selling luminarias?"

"Like crazy. Half of what we made is gone already. And we have orders for several gates, a custom fireplace screen and a decorative railing for a spiral staircase."

"We're doing great, Molly!" Gil called from the far side of the booth. "Wait, do I see the amazing Zach in that wagon?"

She laughed. "In person, for a limited time only."

"Tell him to hold on. Uncle Gil is on his way right after he finishes ringing up this purchase."

"Okay." She sent a startled glance Bret's way. "Uncle Gil?"

"He calls himself that with every kid he meets. He loves kids and they love him. It's his thing."

"I see."

"Zach's ready to bust out of that wagon."

"Go ahead and pick him up. Introduce him to his Uncle Gil."

He smiled. "Good idea. I'll just do that." Walking over to the wagon, he crouched down. "Want out of there, buddy?"

Zach bounced harder and lifted his arms.

"Here we go." Nudging back his hat so he wouldn't hit the kid in the face with the brim, he lifted him out of the wagon. He was a cuddly armful, warm and wiggly. Had he held him before? Maybe not, come to think of it.

He'd scooped him up this time mostly to keep his brother from doing it. Gil had a way with kids, but Bret wasn't ready to let his outgoing brother get his hands on this one.

Carrying the munchkin like a trophy, he intercepted Gil as he came out of the booth. "Zach, meet my brother Gil."

"Hey, there, sport." Gil held out his arms. "Wanna come see your Uncle Gil? Take a little stroll around the fair?"

"Hey, you can't—"

"Just for a few minutes, bro. Marsh and Ella said they'd watch the booth. Whatdya say, big guy? Ready to roam?"

Zach made no move in Gil's direction, just stuck his thumb in his mouth and quietly studied him.

"C'mon, Zach." Gil smiled and wiggled his fingers. "Let's you and me go have some fun."

He looked up at Bret and back at Gil. Then he settled his soft brown gaze on Bret again.

"Your choice, buddy."

A gleam of mischief appeared in his eyes right before he blew a spit-filled raspberry that dribbled down his chin and onto the red bowtie fastened to his green outfit.

Gil chuckled. "Guess he told you."

"Believe it or not, it's a gesture of affection." Bret yanked a bandana out of his back pocket and mopped the bowtie and Zach's face.

"If you say so." His brother tried one more time. "Come on over to your Uncle Gil, Zach. I know where there's a teddy bear with your name on it."

Zach ignored him. Instead he reached up with both hands, patted Bret's cheeks and launched into a stream of baby babble directed solely at him.

The obvious rejection surprised a laugh out of Gil. "I'll be damned. The old Gil McLintock charm is not working on him. That's a first."

"It's probably just because he's more used to me." Had Molly seen or heard any of this? Would she be upset that Zach was clearly bonded with him?

"I think it's more than being used to you. He plain likes you."

"Maybe so."

Gil lowered his voice. "And you like him. You look happy. Seeing you with him makes me wonder if—"

"Hey Bret," Molly called out. Grammy and I are thinking we'd better head over to see Santa pretty soon."

He turned as she came toward them. "We probably should. He's starting in on the raspberries."

"Are you blowing them back at him?"

"No, ma'am. But he's persistent. Any time now he'll be covered with drool."

She glanced at Gil. "Is it okay if Bret leaves for a little while?"

"Molly, take as long as you like. Your brainstorm with the video and the luminarias is the best promo we've ever had. I owe you one."

"That's great to hear."

"It could be a source of income for you, too, if you're interested."

"Oh?" She looked over at Bret.

Just then Zach made a grab for his hat so he took it off. "Several vendors have asked what you'd charge to make a video for them."

"Wow. That's cool. But I have no idea what I'd charge."

"We're keeping a list," Gil said. "You can think about it and follow up if you want. I'm sure you can go online and find out the average going rate for—" He started laughing. "Bret took off his hat so Zach's trying to take off his. He's got it over one eye, now."

"Whoops." Molly stepped forward and tried to get the elf hat on straight, but whenever she took her hands away, Zach made a grab for it. "We'd better get this show on the road before the whole outfit's compromised." She plucked the elf hat off Zach's dark curls. "I'll hang onto this and go fetch Grammy. Be right back."

Gil waited until she was out of earshot. "Anybody seeing you two would assume you're the parents of that kid. I still think it's too soon to make such a huge commitment, but—"

"It's insanity, Gil, and you know it. What if it's just sex, like Mom with our dad?"

"You two have way more in common than our parents did."

"She's not staying."

"You never know. This video thing—"

"Not enough. Town's too small. She'd run out of clients in no time."

"Maybe. Anyway, here they come. Looks like Marsh and Ella are going with you guys, so I need to get back. Have fun with Santa." He ducked into the booth.

Molly showed up pulling the wagon with Grammy, Marsh and Ella behind her.

"We want to come watch," Ella said. "Molly gave us the okay."

Marsh held up his phone. "I just texted Beau. Our timing's perfect. They're taking Maverick over there now. Santa has two knees. We could try getting a shot with both kids."

Bret picked up on the *we* part of that suggestion. Whether Molly wanted this to be a McLintock family picture or not, it was turning out that way.

She gestured toward the wagon. "We can put him back in there if you're getting tired of holding him."

"How about putting my hat in there so he can ride on my shoulders? Might distract him from blowing raspberries."

"Worth a try. I'll bet he'd love it."

"Then here you go."

"Can I wear it?"

"Sure, if you want. Hey, buddy, let's give you a bird's eye view." Grasping him around the waist, he lifted him over his head.

Zach let out a little shriek of excitement.

"This'll be fun, buddy." Clearly nobody had tried this with him because he didn't know what to do with his legs. "Molly, if you can help get his legs... there, perfect. Steady him while I grab his hands. Okay, I've got him. Does he look scared?"

"Oh, no. He looks positively dazzled."

"Excellent. Let's go see Santa."

28

Molly was at least as dazzled as her son. Bret was acting more like a dad every minute. And Zach was eating it up. From his perch above the crowd, he provided a running commentary punctuated with gasps of delight and excited giggles. He'd never been more animated.

Walking beside Bret and Zach surrounded by the cheerful atmosphere of the fair ticked all the boxes for a dream family outing. It would be way too easy to fall under the spell of this fantasy scenario. Better not.

"Did you ask your grandmother for that old straw hat?"

"Not yet."

"Well, if you don't want hers, I'm buying you one. Mine looks even better on you than the old straw one."

"Thanks."

He lowered his voice. "You're kinda quiet. Are you okay?"

"I'm fine. I just... this is feeling so... cozy."

"Too cozy?"

"No. Just right cozy. That's what scares me."

He sighed. "I get it."

"FYI, the video gig could be fun, but it doesn't change things."

"I know. You'd run out of clients in less than a year."

"I'm glad you see that, too. When I went back to get Grammy, Marsh asked me about doing a video for his mobile equine vet website. Grammy lit up when she found out you and Gil have collected a list of prospects."

"I'm sure she did."

"I'll talk to her. Let her know it isn't the answer."

"Good luck with that."

"Thanks."

His voice deepened, sounding almost gruff. "I wish I could see you tonight."

Her breath caught and her heart kicked into high gear. "I wish you could, too."

"What about tomorrow night?"

"Didn't you invite me Grammy and Zach to the ranch for a sleigh ride tomorrow afternoon?"

"Yes, and I realize that means my original plan with the crib isn't feasible. I can't keep you and Zach here with me and send Mrs. J home by herself."

"Or send her back with Zach while I stay here, That just seems wrong."

"I agree. I'll follow you guys back to her house and wait until you tuck him in. I predict he'll go down early after all the excitement and fresh air."

"Probably. And Grammy will offer to cook dinner."

"Let's preempt that. I'd really like for you and me to cook dinner at my place."

Her chest warmed. "Have you been reading my mind?"

"Why?"

"I've been thinking of how much fun that would be ever since we sat across the table at Grammy's that first night. I'd love to cook with you. Let's do it."

"It won't be too cozy?"

"Oh, it will, but let's do it, anyway. I'll mention our plans to Grammy tonight."

"I'll duck out of the fair sometime today and pick up groceries. Any requests?"

"Something fun, not too complicated. I—oh, my goodness! Zach, look! Santa Claus!" As if she'd had to tell him. He'd sucked in a breath the minute they'd turned the corner and encountered the eye-popping display.

"What a great job!" Grammy came up behind them, followed by Marsh and Ella.

Bret laughed. "Welcome to my mother going bananas over Christmas. My mother and the Wenches, I should say."

"And Santa, aka Grandpa Andy," Marsh added.

"Oh, of course!" Ella smacked her forehead. "Grandma Desiree and Grandpa Andy put this together. No wonder it's twice as amazing as last year's. They have a grandchild to impress."

Molly glanced at her. "All this is for Maverick?"

"Not completely, because they've been putting this on for years, but it's definitely the most elaborate one so far."

"Which she won't remember," Marsh said.

"No, but she'll have a gabillion pictures of her first Christmas to look at someday."

"Speaking of that." Molly pulled out her phone. "I need to back up to get a picture. I want the whole thing in the frame." She found a spot that allowed her to capture the entire L'Amour and More Bookshop Christmas display. It took up most of the back wall of the gym.

Santa, dressed in rich red velvet with snowy fur trim, sat on a glittering throne raised above the gym floor by a red carpeted platform with ramps on either side.

A painted backdrop depicted Santa in a red sleigh guiding his reindeer through the night sky with a full moon. Below was a fair representation of Wagon Train's Main Street.

Molly counted six elves, each dressed in a different color of the rainbow, shepherding folks up the ramp and down the other side. At the end of the exit ramp, a tall elf dressed in purple handed each child a book from an assortment on a table nearby. A broad-shouldered cowboy replenished the array whenever the stacks got low.

Tucking her phone away, Molly came back to stand beside the others. "I'll bet that's your mom handing out books."

Bret smiled. "Good call."

"And the cowboy?"

"Our youngest brother Lucky," Marsh said. "He manages the bookstore."

"He's younger than Rance? And he manages the bookstore?"

"He's physically only two hours younger than Rance," Bret said. "Mentally he's years older. His mother died in childbirth and when no one came to claim him, Mom adopted him."

Her breath hitched. "That's quite a story."

"He's quite a guy," Ella said. "One of my favorites."

"You'd better get in line, guys." Marsh gestured toward the crowd gathering. "I just spotted Beau and Jess coming this way. It'd be fun if you can do the baby-on-each-knee thing. Photo-worthy."

"I brought my camcorder, but I don't want to try filming it while I'm up there." She looked at her grandmother. "I didn't think this through, did I?"

"I can film it," Grammy offered.

"You can?"

"Honey, I played with that camcorder for hours before you came to town. Then I carefully repackaged everything so it looked as if it hadn't been opened."

"Then by all means, please get it out. I'm so glad you're able to use it."

"I can also be your assistant when you get your video business up and running."

"Great!" Now wasn't the time to mention that the business would be short-lived. She turned to Bret. "Ready?"

"Should I put him down?"

"I say leave him up there. He seems to love the view."

"Okay."

"Which elf is Colleen, the maker of your socks?"

"She's the blonde in red who's helping kids come down the other side. The one in indigo working with her is Annette. Those are their Wench colors."

"Their *what*?"

"They each have a signature color. Mom's purple, Nancy's yellow, Teresa's orange, Cindy's blue, Annette's indigo. Normally Jess would be there in green, but I'm guessing she got a pass this Christmas so she can focus on Maverick."

"Or not. If she's the elf in green walking beside a tall cowboy carrying a little kid."

He grinned. "That's Jess. And Beau with Maverick." He called out to the couple coming their way. "Cute baby outfit!"

Beau laughed. "I could say the same. So far I've seen at least six of these in the crowd. Hello, there Molly, granddaughter of Mrs. J, and Zach, great-grandson of Mrs. J. This is my highly intelligent wife Jess and my budding genius daughter Maverick."

"I'm happy to meet the folks who inspired this extravaganza. Jess, your costume is something else."

"I couldn't stand not being part of this, so I'll do the parent thing and then Beau's taking Maverick for a while so I can help out here."

Molly peered at the sweet little red-headed girl in Beau's arms. "Is she asleep? In the middle of all this noise?"

He sighed. "She is. She can sleep anywhere, which we both cherish, except for now. Could be awkward when we get to the big moment."

"She'll probably wake up before we get there."

"If not, we'll just prop her up against Santa and photoshop it later," Jess said. "I had no idea it would be so spectacular. By the way, Beau's intro is my fault. He used to introduce us as *my lovely wife Jess and my beautiful daughter Maverick*. I asked him to come up with something that didn't focus on how we looked."

"Consequently, I focus on their brains. They both have top-notch gray matter. Although you can't tell much when they're asleep. That said, I think Maverick looks really intelligent even when she's—"

"Beau, darling, my gray matter tells me we should stop yapping and get in line before twenty more people show up."

"Good point." He gestured for Molly and Bret to go ahead of them.

"No, no," Bret said. "We'll follow you. You're the celebrities of this occasion."

That proved to be true. Once the elves stationed on the ramp spotted Beau, Jess and Maverick, they took turns coming over to chat. Then Bret introduced her to the elves and they fussed over Zach, too.

In fact, he got more attention since Maverick continued to doze in her father's arms. By the time they reached the platform, Molly had learned that Nancy was a movie buff, Teresa made quilts, and Cindy still worked a few hours a week as a hairdresser. For this occasion, she'd dyed her hair red and green.

Molly had a ringside view of Grandpa Andy cradling his fast-asleep granddaughter against his red velvet cloak. She and Jess had nixed Marsh's plan to put both kids on Santa's lap, which could result in two screaming babies.

"Maybe I should poke her," Beau said. "Just so she'll open her eyes."

"Don't you dare, son. Besides, I know what she wants for Christmas."

Jess laughed. "Do you, Dad? Wish you'd tell me."

"Nope. It's between me and Maverick." Leaning down, he gave the little girl a kiss on the cheek and handed her up to Beau.

So sweet. Molly got a little misty-eyed. She'd make it a priority to call her parents today. And do it when Zach was awake so they could see him, if only on her phone's video screen.

Then it was Zach's turn. She pulled out her phone and turned on the camera. Would he get scared and refuse? He hadn't wanted to go to Gil.

Bret lifted him off his shoulders and held him in the crook of his arm so he could look him in the eye. "Want to sit on Santa's lap, Zach?"

Grandpa Andy sat quietly, not saying a word, while Zach took his time. He gazed from Bret to the bearded man in red. Then he looked back at Bret.

"It'll be fun, buddy."

Zach's expression remained solemn. Then he turned and held out his arms to Santa. So far, so good.

She began snapping away, her heart full. Thank heavens Bret had suggested this.

"Well, now, Zach," Grandpa Andy said in a soothing voice, tucking him securely against his side. "What do you want Santa to bring you for Christmas?"

Zach gazed up at him for a couple of seconds. Then he turned and pointed at Bret. "Ga-ga!"

Molly gasped and almost dropped her phone.

29

Bret didn't have a single moment alone with Molly for the rest of the day. Had the Santa incident freaked her out? Maybe not, but he wanted to know for sure.

Late in the afternoon, she and her grandmother came by the booth to announce they were ready to leave. He glanced at Molly. "Can I talk to you for a minute?"

Mrs. J spoke up. "Go ahead, sweetheart. I'll take Zach for a short wagon ride around the area."

"Thanks, Grammy."

Bret turned to his brother. "I'll just be—"

"Take your time." Gil shooed him out of the booth.

Molly smiled as he guided her over to a quiet corner. "Top secret stuff?"

"Just personal stuff. Making sure you weren't bothered by the Santa Claus thing."

"I was startled, but then I realized he didn't know what he was doing."

"Exactly."

"He didn't even understand what Santa was asking. He's never experienced Christmas."

"So true. It was a moment, though. I wanted to say something to you right after we were done there, but—"

"Things got crazy. I wanted to talk to you, too, but it wasn't going to work. Too many people around."

"That's why I wanted to catch you before you left. So we're good?'

"We're good."

"Excellent." He grinned. "Cute as hell, seeing him do that."

"Grammy got it on video, too."

"Great." Reason told him Zach hadn't meant anything by his pointing and babbling. But if that little guy had somehow understood the concept.... His chest ached, but it was a sweet ache. He loved that kid almost as much as he loved—

"You have to be happy about all the business you got today."

He returned to the moment. "I am. Gil's over the moon. Can't stop raving about it. You're his hero."

She laughed. "We'll see if he still thinks so after he and I make those how-to videos. They'll be less fun and more work."

"You're charging him, right?"

"Technically I'm charging McLintock Metalworks, so I'm charging you, too."

"Fine with me. And you'll charge Marsh for the vet video, and Angie for the Handywoman video and Beau for—"

"I'll charge everyone except the Wagon Train Fire Department."

"That I agree with. Cheyenne and the crew will appreciate it. Have you met everyone, then?"

"I think so. And I've talked with each of them quite a bit. Not so much with Clint, because he had to get back to the Fluffy Buffalo, and your mom needed to stick with her job of handing out the books. Did you see the one she gave Zach?"

"I did."

"*Ranch Puppy.* So cute! Looks indestructible."

"Yep. A kid can even chew on it."

"I didn't know M.R. Morrison wrote children's books."

"It's the only one." Maverick's impending birth had inspired the project. Now his mom was hinting at more adventures in store for the rambunctious puppy. "Mom enjoyed meeting you. She told me she can't wait until you and Zach come out tomorrow."

"Speaking of that, did you get to the grocery store?"

"No. When I could see that wouldn't be happening, I checked with Mom. I'm borrowing a few things from her larder. She likes to stock up. As she says, in preparation for the zombie apocalypse."

Molly smiled. "My mom says that, too. Anyway, I'm glad you're not freaked out about the Santa thing, either."

"No, ma'am."

"He is getting attached, though."

"I know. It's my fault. He's so much fun that I allow myself to..." He made a vague gesture, not sure how to finish the comment.

"Be his friend?"

"Yes." He gazed into her warm brown eyes. "I'm his friend. And yours, I hope." And his rebel heart wanted to be much, much more.

"You've been a good friend to me and my son. Without you he would have missed this. He would have missed going out to the ranch tomorrow for a sleighride."

"He's gonna love it." If he told her how much that mattered to him, he ran the danger of spoiling tomorrow's adventure.

"*I'm* gonna love it. I checked the weather and it should be a great day for a sleighride."

"I checked it, too, and—" He glanced over her shoulder. "Here comes your grandmother and Zach. Looks like he fell asleep in the wagon. He's still clutching his book."

She turned around. "He loves it. Doesn't want to let it out of his sight."

"Mom will be tickled to hear that." He should have stolen a kiss before her grandmother showed up. Now it was too late. "In case I haven't told you enough, you look great in my hat."

She reached for it. "You should take—"

"No rush."

"We wore our little guy out." Mrs. J stopped in front of them. "Me, too. But I had a blast, mostly because I got to use the camcorder all day. Thanks, Molly."

"Good thing I turned it over to you. You've got some terrific stuff on there."

"It's so fun to take video and then play it back for people. Everyone loved that. Tomorrow morning I want to do some editing and create something I can give Desiree, since she was passing out books all day and missed a lot."

"We'll do that for sure. Good idea." Molly glanced at Zach. "We'd better get this guy home."

"I'll help you load up." Bret touched her arm. "Wait here a sec. I'll grab my jacket from the booth."

Mrs. J flashed him a smile. "That would be very nice."

He hotfooted it over to the booth where Gil was packing up and chatting with Sky and Penny. "I'll be back in a few minutes, bro." He took his jacket off one of the folding chairs. "I'm gonna help Molly and Mrs. J load their stuff."

"Then take these." Gil pulled out two large shopping bags from under the table. "I've been storing their fair purchases for them. I guess they forgot."

"Obviously they did. Thanks."

"Don't linger, okay? We're all going over to the Buffalo."

"All?" He shoved his arms into the sleeves of his jacket.

"Everybody but Mom," Sky said. "She took Maverick for the night to give Beau and Jess some time off."

"Alrighty then. See you in a few." Grabbing the bags, he hurried back to where he'd left Molly and Mrs. J.

"Oh, our bags! Thank you." She took them and handed over his hat. "Didn't mean to keep it all day."

"I didn't need it."

"Me, either. The sun's not very bright in the gym. I just had fun wearing it."

Should he let her keep it? No, she needed her own, one she chose after trying on a few. He glanced down at Zach, who was still out like a light. They'd tucked a blanket around him for the trip to the car. "We'd better get going so he doesn't overheat."

"Right." Molly reached for the wagon handle.

He beat her to it. "Let me."

"Okay." She had that look in her eyes again, like she'd let him do whatever he wanted... if they were alone.

They would be. That prospect sustained him as he pulled the wagon carefully out of the gym and slowly across the asphalt so it wouldn't jiggle and wake the little guy.

"I loved today," Mrs. J said. "I need more socializing in my life."

"I'll bet Wagon Train's loaded with clubs you could join, Grammy."

"It is. I'll consider it." She beeped open the locks on her Subaru and opened the back door on the passenger side where she'd attached Zach's car seat.

Bret laid down the handle. "I'll put him in."

"I'll accept that offer," Molly said. "He weighs twice as much when he's asleep."

He lifted the sleeping boy out of the wagon and something flopped to the pavement.

"His book," Molly said. "I've got it."

Bret resisted the urge to cuddle the little guy before gently easing him into the car seat. Holding Zach had become one of his favorite things.

By the time he'd fastened him in, Molly had unloaded the wagon and collapsed it. He slid it inside on the floorboard and opened her door.

"Thank you, Bret," Mrs. J called out as she climbed behind the wheel.

"Yes, thank you, Bret." Molly slid onto the front passenger seat.

"My pleasure." Leaning in, he gave her a quick kiss. Then he stepped back and closed the door before he was tempted to give her a second one.

Resisting the impulse to watch them drive away, he turned toward the gym and lengthened his stride. Was this family dinner just because everyone was in town? Or were they looking for a chance to quiz him about Molly?

When he appeared at the booth, Gil rolled his eyes. "Great timing. I'm done."

"I was busy being nice to the lady who gave us a banner sales day."

"Yep, she certainly did. I owe her a beer, but since she's not around, I might as well buy you one. Let's go. I'll drive."

"We could almost walk it."

"Yeah, but we won't. Cowboys don't take walks. Cowboys take pickups." He led the way out to his F-250, the same model as Bret's except his was tan instead of cobalt blue.

Once they were on their way, he turned off the radio, always a signal something serious was coming down. "I need to warn you they've been asking me a bunch of questions about this new relationship."

"To which you've said nothing, I hope?"

"That's correct. I said they'd have to ask you."

"Is that what tonight's about?"

"Partly. Partly it's about consuming food and beer while we find out what everybody's up to."

"But mostly me?"

"Well... yes. And since you've already told Mrs. J your thinking—"

"*Our* thinking."

"Okay, *our* thinking. And considering Mrs. J knows and she's not even kin, and Mom won't be there, I think it's time to discuss it with our nearest and dearest."

"Why?"

"Because after seeing you with Zach and Molly, I'm starting to question the wisdom of our position."

"Gil, she's leaving Wagon Train. My objection won't even come into play."

"You keep saying she's leaving and I keep seeing evidence she might stay."

"Not because of the video thing."

"No, but—"

"You know, maybe it's good that I'll get a chance to say a few things. I'm sure everyone's confused as hell."

"Including you?" Gil parked in front of the Buffalo next to Sky's silver F-250.

"Especially me." He started to open his door, then turned back to his brother. "Thanks for the warning."

"You're welcome. I like her, Bret. I was prepared not to, but she's great."

"I know." He climbed out of the truck and waited for Gil to join him.

"Whatever happens, I've got your back."

"I know that, too." They shared a special bond and he treasured that.

The Buffalo usually went all out for Christmas and this year was no different. Lighted wreaths hung inside the windows facing the street and the rhythmic thump of a live band filtered out to the sidewalk.

A fragrant evergreen wreath decorated the front door, too. When Bret opened it, a wave of music and laughter spilled out along with a tempting aroma.

"Damn, that food smells good." Gil grabbed the heavy door and held it while Bret went in. "I'm starving."

"We sort of forgot to eat lunch." As per tradition, the large wooden buffalo at the entrance wore a white beard and a Santa hat. When Bret walked past, the mascot bellowed *Meeerrrry Chrrrrriiisssmasss.*

Would the buffalo scare Zach or would he love it? In any case, the little guy needed to be introduced to the Fluffy Buffalo. He was old enough to eat the fries. Those would be a hit for sure.

Clint came out from behind the bar and hurried over to meet them. "Everybody's here. I pushed three tables together along the back wall."

"Thanks, bro." Bret unbuttoned his jacket. "The place is hopping."

"Last weekend before Christmas. Always busy. Rance and I are working tonight, but we'll hang out with you as much as we can."

"Appreciate it." Bret gave his shoulder a squeeze.

"What'll you have?"

"Mom's favorite. Hard cider from Apple Grove."

Gil nodded. "Make that two."

"I need to run a pipeline from Apple Grove to the Buffalo. That's all anybody wants anymore. Two hard apple ciders, coming up." He glanced at Bret. "And don't say anything important until I bring your cider over."

"Okay." Bret walked toward his family. His caring, extremely nosy family. He wouldn't have it any other way.

They'd left an empty chair at the head of the cobbled-together dining table. The hot seat, no doubt. He took it. "Looks like you're all fixing to meddle in my business."

Beau laughed. "That's exactly right. We took a vote and everybody loves Molly and Zach.

We're prepared to find ways to coax those two to stick around."

"Like hiring her to make videos for you all?"

"Why not?" Angie sat at the far end of the long table. "Awesome marketing tool."

"No kidding." Clint arrived and set a frosty glass of apple cider in front of Bret and another one in front of Gil. "I asked her to create a video for the Buffalo's website. If she'll make up cards or a flyer, I'll keep a few here to pass on to customers."

"That's great," Bret said, "but we're not a big enough town for her to build that into a career, even if she wanted to. I'm not sure she does." He picked up the cider. "Thanks, bro."

"But a video business would be a start," Marsh said. "She's a talented lady. We might be small, but that doesn't mean there aren't opportunities here. Especially if a person is motivated to stay."

"And that's where you come in, big brother." Angie sent a big smile down the length of the table.

"Why is there a problem?" Cheyenne frowned. "Are you gun shy after what happened with Jen last Christmas? Because Molly's nothing like—"

"It's not that."

"Then what is it?" Sky nudged back his hat and gazed at him over the rim of his beer mug. "Gil says you have no intention of getting serious about Molly."

"Which, by the way, is a joke," Kendall announced. "You're serious about her, dude. I could tell the minute Cheyenne and I walked into the shop yesterday with that big ol' bag of condoms."

Beau grinned. "You might want to repeat that last part, Kendall. And say it a little louder. Some folks at the other tables didn't quite catch it."

"Sorry. I should have said the big ol' bag of *Rance's* condoms. Did you all see those goofy things? I have some pictures on my phone if anyone—"

"I think we're straying from the topic." Sky's voice sounded funny, like he was trying hard not to laugh. He cleared his throat. "For better or worse, we're in this together. We'll support you no matter what, but...."

"You're all scratching your heads. I get it. My apologies for that." Taking a deep breath, he glanced over at Gil, who'd taken the chair on his right.

Gil gave him a nod.

"Years ago, Gil and I had a talk about whether we'd ever get married. We both said we'd like to, and we wanted to make it last. After watching Mom's pattern, we decided the key was getting to know someone really well before you had kids with them."

"So why not have a long courtship with Molly before making it official and having more kids?" Jess's earnest suggestion sounded adorable coming from a woman dressed in a green elf suit.

"Partly because that seems unfair to Zach. He'd get attached to me and if we ended up not making that commitment...."

Jess sighed. "Good point. But I think you would make it. I got such good vibes from you two while we stood in line waiting for Santa."

"Unfortunately, an extended courtship wouldn't work for Molly. She promised her late husband she'd get married soon and try to get pregnant so Zach will have a brother or sister. She's an only and so was her husband. They didn't want that for Zach."

"Wow. That shines a whole different light on things."

"Now I'm worried for Molly," Angie said. "What if she marries somebody in a hurry and picks the wrong guy?"

"What if I'm the wrong guy?"

"I can speak to this," Penny said. "I came so close to marrying the wrong guy. I shudder to think of it. But Bret, you're the right guy. She'll never find anybody better than you."

"Exactly!" Kendall pointed a finger at him. "I totally agree with Penny. Molly would work out for you, Bret. Think of how cool she was about the condom tree."

Beau laughed. "This conversation just keeps getting better. Wish I'd thought to record it."

"Me, too." Clint tucked the drinks tray under his arm. "If you'd offered to record it, I wouldn't have to stand here, unable to tear myself away while Rance is behind the bar flipping breakables."

"For what it's worth, Penny and I were complete strangers when we met," Sky said. "But in a few days—"

"Hey, Captain Obvious." Beau waved a hand in the air. "Everybody's a complete stranger when you meet them. That's the definition of a—"

"Okay, okay. I'm just saying that we didn't grow up together. We knew almost nothing about each other. We had no basis for falling in love except after a few days… we just knew."

"There are exceptions," Bret said. "You're lucky."

"No, I'm Lucky. He's Sky." Their little brother deadpanned the line. He never made jokes. The table went completely silent. Then everybody cracked up.

When the laughter and side comments trailed off, Beau leaned forward so he could look straight down the table at Bret. "I get what you're saying, bro. Your conclusion about relationships is perfectly logical. But here's the problem. You're trying to use logic to deal with love and sex. And I'm here to tell you, that dog won't hunt."

30

Zach woke up while Molly was taking him out of his car seat. Emerging from his dreams, he made soft cooing noises as she gathered him into her arms.

"I hear Zach," Grammy said as she opened the back door on the driver's side.

"He's still sleepy. I'll take him in, make him a quick dinner and give him a bottle."

"I'll run ahead and unlock the front door for you, sweetheart."

"Thanks, Grammy." She nudged the car door shut with her hip and walked out of the ancient garage into a peaceful, twilight world. Cheerful holiday decorations glowed from porches and windows up and down the street. Grammy and Grandpa had chosen a great neighborhood.

The Christmas spirit washed over her for the second time today, and she hugged Zach's warm little body close. She hadn't spent much time carrying him today.

He'd either been in the wagon, with Bret, or with some other member of his family. They'd welcomed her and Zach as if they expected this romance to go somewhere. She had moments when she wished the same thing. But Bret didn't have the same wish.

Zach barely stayed awake long enough to eat his supper. While her grandmother warmed a bottle, Molly took him upstairs and got him ready for bed.

Just as she finished putting on his sleeper, Grammy came up with his bottle. "Figured you'd be ready."

"Thanks." She settled into the rocker with Zach in her lap. "He'll be asleep soon."

"Where's his book?"

"I tucked it in one of the bags from the fair, if you want to look for it."

"I do. I'm fascinated that a crusty old guy like M.R. Morrison wrote a charming book for little kids."

"Maybe he wrote it for a grandchild."

"That's a great theory. He's old enough to have one by now. I'll go start the toasted cheese sandwiches. See you in a few."

"I won't be long."

Zach was asleep before he finished his bottle. She put him to bed and headed down to the kitchen. "I feel like I'm at Mom's. She always fixed tomato soup and toasted cheese sandwiches after a long day."

"I wonder where she got that?" Grammy smiled as she handed her a spatula. "I'll dish the soup if you'll get the sandwiches."

"Deal." When she was settled at the kitchen table with food and a cup of herbal tea, she let out a happy sigh. "It's nice to relax." She glanced at the little book lying on the table. "I see you found it."

"Yep. I'm gonna research it, see if the publisher's website says whether there will be more."

"See, that's another fun thing that came out of going today. Zach got that book."

"It's clever. Desiree beat me to the punch. I have a couple books to put in his stocking, but he got his first book from her. Which is fine. Of course she'd have an M.R. Morrison new release. She stocks everything he writes."

"Now I want to go see her bookstore."

"I haven't been in for months. This fair was a wakeup call for me. I've been too isolated."

"Gonna join a club?"

"I've been thinking about that. I want something bigger, more of a challenge."

"Like what?" Molly took a bite of her sandwich. Yummy. Tasted just like her mother's.

"Like opening a bed and breakfast."

"What?" She put down her sandwich. "Where?"

"Here, of course. Oh, don't worry. I'm not talking about doing it next week. It'll take months to get everything ready. We'd need a second bathroom upstairs, for one thing. And those two back bedrooms haven't been cleaned and repainted in years."

Molly's tired brain wasn't handling this well, but she snagged one significant word out of the many coming out of Grammy's mouth. "You said *we*."

"Did I?"

"Yes, you said we'd need a second bathroom upstairs."

"Oh, well, of course I would love to have you throw in with me. That would be fabulous. But whether you do or not, I'm charging ahead."

"Grammy, if this is part of a plan to give me an income so I can stay here—"

"I swear it's not. I'll hire someone to help me run it if you don't want to. It's a dynamite idea. This is a cute little town and I have a beautiful house. We don't have any B&Bs in Wagon Train. It would be a gold mine."

Molly studied her. No secret smile, just a firm set to her mouth. Behind her tortoise shell glasses, her eyes gleamed with determination and excitement. "You're serious about this."

"Serious as a librarian shelving rare books."

"I have to admit it's brilliant. You'd make a wonderful B&B hostess."

"I know I would. Ever since your grandfather died I've been floundering, not sure what came next for me. I had no family living here until you and Zach moved in, and you may or may not stay. If you do, I hope you'll consider helping me with this."

"Of course I would. If I stayed here, that is, but that's—"

"Up in the air. Or in the stars. But if you and Zach do leave, I'll have this to keep me busy. I won't have to worry about being lonely."

Molly got up and gave her a hug. "It's a wonderful idea and props to you for coming up with a project that makes you excited."

"I'm proud of myself, too. Now eat your food before it gets cold."

"Yes, ma'am." She sat down again and picked up her soup spoon. "I've been worried about how you'd take it when Zach and I left."

"Assuming you do."

"I think I have to. Zach's getting more attached to Bret. The longer I stay here, the more Zach will miss him when we leave."

"He'll miss me, too, you know."

"I know, but we'll keep in touch. We'll visit every chance I get. And now that we can use our phones to see people as well as — oh, my goodness. I promised myself I'd call Mom and I haven't done it." She glanced at the kitchen clock. "It's only a little after eight there. I'll call right after I finish eating."

"I'm sure they're still up."

"I'll grab my phone so I don't forget." She hurried into the foyer, took it out of her coat pocket and tapped it. Silly her, she was hoping for a text from Bret.

And she had a text. Heart thumping, she opened it. But the text wasn't from Bret. She carried the phone into the kitchen, reading as she walked.

"A message?"

"From the hotel I interviewed with in Colorado Springs this past summer, the one I told you was so amazing."

"I remember. You said it was even nicer than the El Capitan."

She sat down, finished the long text and glanced up. "The person they hired instead of me just announced this afternoon that she has a family crisis and will be leaving the first of the year. The job is mine if I want it. The CEO would love an immediate answer, but she's giving me until Christmas. After that she'll contact the next person on the list."

Her grandmother swallowed. "See there? You never know when the Universe will send you a gift. What a great opportunity."

"Oh, Grammy." Her chest hurt. "You don't have to say that. You can be upset."

"But it's your dream job, in a place that has mountains, and it's a big city, so you'll have a much better chance of finding—"

"And you know what? The idea of searching for Mr. Right sounds awful now."

"Because you've already found him?"

"No, I haven't. I've screwed up. I'm in love with the wrong guy."

* * *

Molly was prepared for Rowdy Ranch to be big. It was, but in a subtle way. The one-story ranch house had a sizeable footprint, but it nestled into the snowy landscape without dominating it. The long front porch decorated with pine boughs and red ribbon was striking without a hint of ostentation.

The outbuildings also blended in. Only the barn made a bold statement, as if announcing its importance as the lynchpin of the operation. Dark red with white trim, it boasted a large wreath hung between the double doors at ground level and a smaller set of doors into the hayloft.

"Oh, Molly, look at that sleigh!" Grammy braked the Subaru and rested her hands on the steering wheel.

"I'm looking. It's like something out of a fairy tale." Just like the broad-shouldered man working with Sky to hitch up the very big horse to the sleigh. No prince would make her heart race like that cowboy could.

"And the horse!"

"He's stunning. And *huge*."

"He could be a Belgian. Your grandpa used to shoe one of those. The caramel coat and cream mane and tail are common. And he's wearing bells on his harness! What fun."

"Sleighbells! Talk about a Christmas adventure." Molly glanced over her shoulder. The backwards facing car seat kept her from seeing Zach's face, but he was awake. He'd been talking to himself throughout the trip and he'd fallen silent when the car stopped. "Ready to go for a sleigh ride, Zach?"

"Ba-ba! Ba-ba ga-ga!"

Grammy laughed. "I think that's a yes." She took her foot off the brake. "I'd better park this buggy." She drove slowly over to the right of the barn.

"Have you ever been out here?"

"No. Your grandpa was here many times to shoe their horses and Desiree invited me, but I was so busy I didn't make it out. We were all busy back then, including Desiree."

"At the bookstore?"

"She used to work there, but now Lucky handles it all." Grammy parked between Sky's silver truck and Bret's blue one.

"That bookstore must be profitable."

"That's not where the money comes from. No one opens a bookshop hoping to get rich. It's a labor of love." She switched off the motor.

"But she doesn't raise horses or cattle, or take in guests, so where—"

"Rumor has it she inherited a pile of money and invested it wisely. I don't know if that's true or not. And speaking of Desiree, here she comes." Grammy climbed out.

Molly grabbed Zach's snowsuit from the bag at her feet. He couldn't wear it in the car, but he'd need it for the sleighride.

Opening the back door, she laid the snowsuit on the back seat. "Hey, kiddo. Let's spring you from that contraption."

"Ga-ga!" He strained at the harness while keeping a tight grip on his book.

"Need any help?"

Bret's deep voice startled her. The warm and caring tone loosened a torrent of emotion she'd been stuffing ever since last night's text. She longed to throw herself into his arms, but she had to settle for looking into his beautiful eyes.

"Molly? Is something—"

"I got a job offer."

31

The air left his lungs. "Where?"

"Colorado Springs." She ducked back into the car and fumbled with Zach's harness while he wiggled in the seat.

Colorado Springs. He'd been there once. About 700 miles. His stomach hollowed out. So far away. Too far.

Zach struggled to get loose while waving his book around. "Ga-ga ba-ba!"

"I see that, buddy. Great book." Molly seemed to be losing her battle with those straps. He laid his hand on her shoulder. "Let me."

"Sure. Okay. I'm making a mess of it."

"Hold my hat, please." She'd worn the ratty straw one. She must have put it on today because he liked it. And she was leaving. Colorado Springs had mountains. And a shitload of eligible men.

Don't think about it. He concentrated on extracting an excited little boy from a car seat that didn't seem to want him to leave. Zack waved the book around and smacked him a couple of times in the head. Not on purpose. He didn't have that kind of aim yet.

"Hey, son, want to step back and let a pro take the field?"

"Just got it, Mom, but thanks." He lifted Zach out, book and all. But the kid only had on overalls and a shirt. "He doesn't look ready for a sleighride, though." Quickly unbuttoning his jacket, he tucked the little guy inside.

"His snowsuit's lying beside the car seat.," Molly said. "Let me have him and the suit."

"Okay." He didn't want to let go of him. Molly was leaving. Zach was leaving. He transferred him to Molly and she quickly laid him on the front passenger seat.

He stepped back and his mom came to stand beside him as Molly expertly worked Zach into the suit, coaxing him to transfer the book from one hand to the other.

His mom lowered her voice. "Is that my book?"

"Yes, ma'am. He's been nuts about it ever since you gave it to him."

"That's it. He's officially part of the family."

He chuckled, but her comment made him sad. She would have loved getting to know Zach. Now that wouldn't be happening.

"Hey, Molly," his mom said. "Bret says Zach's really enjoying the book."

"He loves it." Molly zipped the suit and pulled the hood over his head. "I can't get him to put it down."

"Well, that's gratifying."

"He looks at the pictures, but he also chews on it." She scooped him up.

"No worries. It was designed for that."

Molly straightened and glanced around. "Where's Grammy?"

"She went to talk with Sky and admire Thor. Turns out draft horses are one of her interests. So I came to see what was holding things up back here."

"The car seat didn't want to let go of him, but I think we're all set, now."

"Before we head over to the sleigh, would you let me take him for a little tour of the barn first? Kids usually love that."

"Sure. You can take him if he'll go to you, or if he won't, I'll just carry him while you direct the tour."

"I think he'll come to me." Desiree held out her arms. "Let's go, big guy. I have some cool stuff to show you."

"Ga-ga!" Zach launched himself at her.

Laughing, she caught him in her arms. "That's what I like to hear." Her voice took on a lilting rhythm. "We'll say hello to *Trig*ger and *Butter*milk and Di*ablo* and maybe get a *cook*ie...."

Zach gazed at her in fascination. Then he swung the book in the direction of her face. "Ba-ba."

She dodged the blow easily. "Let's not read the book now. We can do that on the sleigh ride." She turned to them. "You guys want to go, too?"

He looked at Molly.

She gave him a little smile and glanced at his mom. "Thanks, but I have something to discuss with Bret."

"Then we'll see you over by the sleigh in a few minutes." She whisked Zach away.

Molly followed their progress into the barn. "Wow. He practically leaped into her arms."

"You've now seen one of the reasons my mother had so many children. She adores them. They sense that and adore her right back."

"Seems so."

"Also, notice that she didn't ask. It was *let's go.* She expects compliance. She usually gets it."

"Good parenting tip. I'll remember that."

He took a deep breath. "Tell me about Colorado Springs."

"The hotel is gorgeous. I'd have a place to live on the property, daycare for Zach, full benefits. The CEO and I think alike on how to treat guests." The details were all positive but she recited them without enthusiasm.

"Was this a place you'd sent a resume to?"

"No. It's a hotel where I interviewed this summer. Ironically, I didn't get the job because they wanted someone with videography experience."

"And now you have that. Talk about good luck."

"She doesn't know that yet. She's offered to pay for training and I'd take her up on it. There's plenty more to learn."

"The other person didn't work out?"

"She did, but she's quitting the first of the year. Family emergency."

"The first of the year? Then you'll—" He had to pause and clear his throat. Felt like he had something stuck in it. Yeah, like his heart. "You'll need to start right away."

"Yes. The CEO sent me a text last night. She'd like to know ASAP, but she's giving me until Christmas for an answer. On the twenty-sixth, she'll contact the next candidate on the list."

"You're taking it, right?"

"I'd be a fool not to. It's exactly what I'm looking for."

"Sounds like it." He gazed into her dark eyes and saw nothing but confusion. "Molly, if you'd landed this job six months ago, you would have been over the moon."

"Yes, I would have. But I didn't get it. Then I moved here and met you."

"I'm just a sideroad on your way to rebuilding your life."

"A *sideroad*? Take that back. You are not now, nor have you ever been a *sideroad.* You—"

"Hey." He drew her into his arms. "Maybe that's the wrong word, but we knew from the start that we... well, maybe not the start, but—"

"I care about you."

The bands around his chest tightened. "I care about you, too. That's why I hope you take this job. It has everything. You'll be doing work that challenges you in a setting you love." He couldn't make himself mention the husband-hunting project.

"You're right, of course." Her brow furrowed. "But—"

"We knew this day would come."

"There's something else."

"Let me guess." He needed to tackle this. Face the dragon. "You have an old boyfriend who lives in Colorado Springs."

"Oh, God, no! I can't even think about that right now. Yuck."

"I don't know if that makes me feel better or worse."

"Same here." She took a breath. "Grammy's opening a bed and breakfast."

"She *is*?" He stared at her. "Boy, she *really* wants you to stay. I don't think I realized the lengths she'd—"

"It's not about me. It's about her."

"And you believe that?"

"I do. She'll do it whether I go or stay. Of course if I were to stay, she'd want me to help her run it."

"Well, duh. I still think she—"

"Nope. She's like you. She's urging me to take this fabulous job. That's why I'm telling you, so you won't think it's a maneuver on her part. She's ready to enter a new chapter in her life."

"And so are you." Damn, this hurt like hell.

She held his gaze. Still a lot of uncertainty going on there.

"Molly, this is a good thing. A very good thing."

"I won't get to make those videos for your family."

"They'll understand. They'll be happy for you."

She looked away. "We should go. Everybody could be over there waiting for us."

He nodded. "And if I kiss you, I might never stop."

"You can kiss me tonight."

"Don't worry. I will." He let her go, but he held her hand as they walked around the tailgate of Sky's truck and over to the sleigh. His mom and Zach weren't there yet.

Mrs. J clearly didn't mind. She was chatting up a storm with his brother. She turned to them with a smile. "I had no idea Sky has a connection to a ranch in Apple Grove. The Buckskin sounds like a wonderful place to visit."

"Yes, ma'am. I haven't been there yet, but it's on my list."

"You're all welcome to come when Penny and I go over with Mom between Christmas and New Year's."

"I just might take you up on that." He needed a distraction to help him deal with Molly's departure. His comment earned him a glance from Mrs. J, though. She'd likely figured out Molly had told him about the job.

"We could caravan over there." Sky continued cheerfully, since he wasn't in the know. "You could take Molly, Zach and Mrs. J."

"Sounds great, Sky." Mrs. J gave Molly's arm a squeeze. "We'll let you know."

"We're on our way!" His mom came out of the barn holding Zach. "Sorry if we made you wait."

"No worries," Sky said. "We're just talking about our trip to Apple Grove. These guys might like to go along."

His mom beamed at them. "Well, sure, why not?"

"Alrighty, then. Time to climb into this buggy. Figure out where you all want to sit and we'll do this thing."

Mrs. J spoke up first. "This was Bret's idea, so I think he and Molly should sit facing the front."

His mom nodded. "Absolutely. You and I will take the other side. But the big question is, who gets the pleasure of holding Zach?"

Mrs. J took the lead again. "I get to hold him all the time. So does Molly. Maybe you and Bret can trade off."

"Works for me." She turned to him. "Bret?"

He gave her a smile. "Me, too." A more noble son would let his mother have Zach the whole ride. But encouraging Molly to take this job had used up every noble drop in his body. He wanted his share of holding that little guy on his first sleighride.

And they were off, one green lap robe tucked around him, Molly and Zach, and a second one keeping Mrs. J and his mom warm and cozy. The bells on Thor's harness jingled rhythmically and Mrs. J began singing *Jingle Bells.*

They all joined in. Zach bounced in time to the music as he babbled his own version of the song. Holding him secure with one arm, Bret reached for Molly's hand under the lap robe.

She gave his hand a squeeze. Turning his head, he met her gaze. Uh-oh. There was no mistaking the warmth in her dark eyes. No wonder she was confused about the job offer. She was in love with him.

32

"I'll never forget that sleighride." Surrounded by the scent of evergreen, Molly settled into the comfy seat of Bret's truck as he pulled away from Grammy's house. "Or my first time chopping down a Christmas tree."

"You did well."

"It wasn't a thick trunk. I'll bet you chose a smaller one on purpose."

"I did, but it worked out since we needed to put it in the cab instead of the back."

They'd wanted to keep it from getting covered in snow, which it would have been by now. Flakes had started falling when they'd come back to the ranch and had continued, light but steady, since then. The windshield wipers swept back and forth clearing it away.

"Sure smells good."

"Sure does. And because it's small, it won't take long to decorate." He paused. "Assuming we still want to do that. We could skip it."

"Why would we do that?"

He glanced her way. "Why do you think?"

"Ah. Because you'd rather spend the time doing something else."

"Yes, ma'am."

Her relaxed mood, lulled by the fragrant tree and *Walking in a Winter Wonderland* on the radio, evaporated in the heat of his gaze. "Do you still want to cook?"

"We'll have to if we want to eat."

"What are we having?"

"Lasagna."

"Mmm. Good choice."

"I'm cheating a little. Mom gave me a jar of Marybeth's sauce, which is a major part of making it."

"But it'll still be fun putting it together."

"I'm going for fun and fast."

"I thought we'd talked about doing it slow and sexy."

"We did, but my priorities have changed since then."

"Bret, I'm not leaving tomorrow."

"Feels like it." Then he took a deep breath. "Sorry. I won't... I promise not to—"

"Complain?"

"Complain, whine, in general make this all about me. You've just scored a major victory in a competitive market. Your interview impressed this hotel owner if you were the first person she contacted."

"We did hit it off, but the other applicant had the videography skills and a little more experience."

"What time did she text you?"

"A little after five. She found out she was losing her manager sometime yesterday afternoon."

He was silent for a moment. "Why not text her back and take the job?"

"You mean now?"

"Now."

Her stomach twisted. "Because then I'm leaving for sure. Once I accept it, there's no turning back."

"But you said you'd be a fool not to take it."

"I know."

"Do you think a few more days will make it easier to leave me?"

"That's what I'm hoping."

He groaned. "Molly, I'm so sorry." He reached for her hand. "This is my fault. That first night, when I found out about Zach, I should've ended it."

She took his hand in both of hers and held it to her cheek. "It's not all your fault. You couldn't resist my womanly charms."

"So true."

They rode the rest of the way just listening to the Christmas carols. Talking wasn't helpful. But touching was, so she kept holding his hand. Making love to him would help even more.

When he pulled up in front of his cabin, she released her hold so he could switch off the engine. "Do you need to get the tree out and put it in water?"

"Not right now. It'll be nicely refrigerated out here."

"We can wait on dinner if you want."

"I want."

"You left lights on in the house this time."

"Lights on, covers turned back, condoms on the nightstand. Stay put, okay? It's always slippery right there for some reason."

She waited for him. He helped her down and wrapped an arm around her shoulders as they hurried into the house.

As he took her coat, she glanced at the fireplace. Logs on the grate, place settings on the coffee table. "Are we eating in front of the fire?"

"Thought we would." He shrugged out of his jacket and hung it on the rack along with his hat.

"You really prepped for tonight."

"I'm glad I did."

Curious comment. "Why?"

"I'm just... glad. Wait here." He headed down the hall and into his darkened bedroom.

Then light flickered. He was lighting candles. She pressed a hand to her heart.

He'd had very little time between the end of the fair and the sleighride, and he'd used all of it to set up a romantic evening. How would she find the strength to give him up?

He came toward her. "All set." He led her down the hall and into the room.

"Oh, my goodness." The covers weren't turned down anymore. He'd flung them aside. A pair of breathtaking luminarias, one on each bedside table, cast a glow on the snowy sheets. The intertwined design of holly leaves and berries left very little of the pipe. The twin luminarias radiated light, beauty… and love.

She turned to him. "They're incredible."

"They're yours. Merry Christmas."

Her throat tightened. "I guess you know I'm in love with you."

"I do." He began tenderly undressing her. "And I'm in love with you. And we'll… we'll just deal with it."

"How?"

"We just will." He peeled off the rest of her clothes, picked her up and laid her gently on the bed. "But right now, I need you, Molly." He stripped off his shirt and nudged off his boots.

"I need you, too."

"Then let's take care of that, at least." He finished undressing, his magnificent body caressed by filtered candlelight.

He made quick work of rolling on the condom. Then he was there, his lips teasing hers, his furred chest brushing her taut nipples, the blunt tip of his cock seeking, finding, thrusting deep.

She wrapped him in her arms and rose to meet those thrusts. He loved her. Each stroke confirmed it. Even if she had nothing else to hold onto, she'd hold onto this.

When she let go, when she surrendered to the fierce pace of his loving, she captured the joy and tucked it away in her heart. His cries of completion would forever live in her memory. She was loved by Bret McLintock.

* * *

Making lasagna with Bret didn't live up to her fantasy, but she wasn't surprised. They were both in a funky mood, thrown off-balance by her job offer.

While it was baking, they drank wine in front of a crackling fire. He'd dressed in sweatpants and a T-shirt for making dinner, and she'd borrowed an identical outfit. His clothes swam on her, but they were soft and cozy.

While he put another log on the fire, she poured them each more wine. "I didn't think about needing something to lounge around in."

"That's okay. We worked it out."

"How was business at the fair this morning? I should have asked you sooner."

"That's okay. You've had a lot going on. Sales were good today, too. We sold the last of the luminarias and have orders for more, including some with year-round designs. Some folks want to use them on their porch in the summertime. Put in a citronella candle and you have a mosquito deterrent."

"Hey, you could make some with a mosquito design!"

"Um, no. That's a terrible idea."

"Is it? They'd know immediately what they were for. You could even include the citronella candles."

"Have you ever looked at a mosquito? All the spindly parts? I'm good with a torch, but I'm not that good."

"You are good with a torch. The luminarias you made for me are so delicate."

He winced. "Let's not say *delicate.* Let's say *intricate.* That's a word a manly blacksmith can live with. *Delicate*? Not so much."

"I'll keep that in mind. It's a wonderful gift, regardless of how I describe it. You got the jump on me. I don't have—"

"Say no more. I wasn't sure these were appropriate, given that we're in some unspecified area when it comes to gift exchanges."

"They're appropriate. I'll cherish them. They took a lot of effort. I know because I filmed you making the others."

He smiled. "Just trying to impress you."

"You succeeded." She held his gaze.

The arresting blue-green slowly darkened. His chest heaved. "Lasagna should be ready."

They ate in front of the fire, but the casual atmosphere didn't hold. Something was going on with him. She waited until they'd both finished. "Okay, Bret. What's up?"

"That's a leading question, lady."

"I'm not trying for sexy talk. I'm serious. Something's on your mind."

He stared into the fire. "I wasn't planning to say this yet."

"Say what?"

"We have to stop seeing each other."

Shock gave her brain freeze. "Huh?"

"You need to accept this amazing offer. You're stalling because of me." His jaw tightened and a pulse beat at his temple. "I need to get out of your life so you can focus on what's clearly your best move."

The brain freeze quickly moved through the rest of her body. "Th-that's it?"

He scooted around and took her icy hands in his. "I don't see any other way." His expression was achingly earnest. "I'm not good for you, Molly."

"Yes, you are!"

"No, I'm not. I'm bowing out. It's the right thing to do. Tonight's the last—"

"Then take me home." She pulled her hands away and stood. "I'll get dressed."

"Molly, I didn't mean you had to—"

"If you're calling it off, I don't want to stick around." She began shaking. Time to get the hell out of Dodge before she fell apart. She gestured toward the fire. "Bank that so it doesn't burn down your cabin while you drive me back to Grammy's."

"But—"

"I mean it! I'll be ready in five minutes."

"Okay."

It took her less than that to wrench off his sweatpants and T-shirt, pull on her clothes and march back into the living room.

She accepted his help with her coat, although that wasn't so easy. His touch and his scent tempted her to grab him and never let go. But he didn't want that.

They drove back to town in total, apocalyptic silence. He'd switched off the radio the moment he'd started the truck. When they arrived at Grammy's he insisted on walking her to the door, despite her protests.

She pulled out her key and turned to him. "I forgot my luminarias."

"I'll see that you get them. Molly—"

"So long, Bret. It's been..." She couldn't finish.

"For me, too." His voice was hoarse.

"See you." She unlocked the door and went inside. Then, like a fool, she went to the window in the parlor and looked out through the branches of the Christmas tree.

His sat in his truck for a very long time. Finally, he started the engine and drove off. If only she could cry. But she had no tears. She had nothing but emptiness. This was for the best, right?

33

The next morning during breakfast, Molly explained to Grammy that Bret had called it off and why he had. "In the light of day, I can see it as a noble gesture, even if it hurt like hell."

"It was noble, sweetheart, but sad. For both of you." Grammy gazed at her, sympathy shining in her eyes. "I'm sorry."

"Me, too." She heaved a sigh. "But I knew we were on borrowed time."

"Are you going to call the CEO and accept the job?"

She shook her head. "Not yet. I plan to, but I need some space to process everything and make sure I'm totally on board."

"Good idea."

"I'm also going to call Colleen."

"Colleen from the Wenches?"

"Yep."

"For what?"

"On Saturday we had some time to chat. She told me that crocheting and knitting relaxes her and creates lovely things to give away, like the socks Bret has."

"What socks?"

"The ones… well, it's not important. But she offered to teach me how to do some simple knitting, so I'm going to try that. She also said it helps her think things through."

Grammy nodded. "I can see how it might. Just let me know when you need me to watch Zach."

"Thanks, Grammy. I'll see if she's available today."

Colleen was not only available, she'd stocked in the exact colors and type of yarn Molly needed for what she had in mind. Colleen wouldn't take any money for either the lesson or the yarn. By that evening, Molly was slowly knitting a scarf in shades of red and green.

For the next three days, she worked on it when Zach was napping and after he went down for the night. With some phone support from Colleen whenever she got in trouble, she made good progress.

Four days into it and she was convinced she'd have it done by Christmas Eve. True to Colleen's prediction, the repetitive motion helped her untangle all the conflicting thoughts swirling in her head.

On Friday morning, she sat with Grammy at the kitchen table, eager to make her announcement. She'd put it off while she'd fed Zach some of her grandmother's oatmeal and had eaten a bowl of it herself. Now Zach was busy with a trayful of Cheerios.

She glanced across the table at Grammy, who sat with her coffee reading the *Sentinel.* "I have something to tell you."

Grammy looked up and adjusted her glasses. "What's that, sweetheart?"

"I'm not taking the job."

Her grandmother's eyes widened. "Why not?"

"I'd rather stay here and manage your B&B."

She gasped. "Are you sure? Because that's a hell of an opportunity and my B&B won't be nearly as—"

"It's exactly what I want. I thought managing a hotel in a major city was my path because I was so used to that environment. But I've fallen in love with this town and I can't imagine living anywhere else. I've only been here since Thanksgiving and yet it feels more like home than anywhere I've ever lived."

Grammy took off her glasses and wiped her eyes.

"Are you crying?"

She nodded. "It's happy tears."

Molly stood and so did Grammy. They met in the middle and hugged, both gulping and sniffling while Zach banged on his highchair and scattered Cheerios everywhere.

"Okay, okay. That's enough blubbering." Grammy backed away. "Sit back down. I have a question."

"Ask away."

"What about Bret?"

"You mean the guy I'm knitting the scarf for?"

"That's what you're doing? Knitting him a scarf?"

"It was the easiest thing. I couldn't manage a sweater. Or even socks. But I wanted to give him something I'd made because he gave me those luminarias. I guess they're still at his house."

"No, they're tucked in the back of the pantry."

"He brought them here?"

"He said he'd promised to."

"I know, but how did I miss him? I haven't been anywhere except — did he come when I was at Colleen's?"

"Yes. I think he was disappointed not to see you, but I had no idea when you'd be back, so he gave me the luminarias and left."

"Why didn't you tell me?"

"You were so... emotional. I decided to put them away for the time being."

"That's probably for the best. They would have made me cry."

"Thought so."

"But I'm way better, now that I've decided not to leave. I can't wait to start brainstorming ideas for the B&B."

"Me, either." Grammy's face seemed lit from within. "It'll be awesome. But you haven't answered my question about Bret."

"I'm still working through that situation. I have a little more to do on his scarf, so maybe the answers will come to me."

"He's so in love with you. He told me so when he dropped off the luminarias."

"He did?" She got warm shivers. "And I love him, too. It's just that our situation is complicated. I want to give him the scarf for Christmas, so I'll probably contact him Sunday and ask if I can see him, let him know I'm staying, and take it from there."

Grammy smiled. "That sounds lovely."

* * *

Bret finally had to decorate the tree or forget it. It was the twenty-third, for crying out loud. He hauled out the boxes and started, but his heart wasn't in it. His heart was AWOL, in fact, residing in a quaint Victorian on a quiet street in Wagon Train.

The call from his mother was a welcome reprieve from a depressing task. "Hey, Mom."

"You know the job you told me Molly was taking?"

"Yes."

"She turned it down."

"She *what*?" He grabbed onto the back of the couch as his world tilted.

"Elvira just called me, and you are not to divulge that to anyone. As far as you know, that call never happened."

"Who's Elvira? Oh, wait, that's—"

"Mrs. J."

"Are you saying Molly told Mrs. J that she isn't taking the job?"

"She did. This morning."

He glanced at the clock. Almost two. Molly hadn't called him, though, had she? Why not? And why wasn't she taking the job? "Mom, somebody needs to talk to her. She has to take that job. It's perfect."

"Evidently not. She's already contacted the hotel and turned it down."

"That makes no sense. I backed away so she could stop thinking about me and start thinking about what a great job she had waiting for her."

"Instead she realized that this town has become her home and she wants to stay and help Elvira run the B&B."

"Did Mrs. J talk her into that idea? Because Molly needs a creative challenge, and I don't see how running a B&B in Wagon Train even begins to compare with managing an entire hotel in Colorado Springs."

"Elvira didn't talk her into it. She made sure to avoid discussing the B&B this week. It was Molly's decision. And you of all people should know that starting a business from scratch is a huge challenge."

Oh. Right. He and Gil had sweat bullets over the business loan, the modifications to the shop, the possibility of losing their shirts. Big challenge, and it remained one, probably would for some time.

"Bret, are you still there?"

"Sorry. I'm here. I was thinking. You have a point."

"Of course I do. I'm your mother."

He laughed. "Any more words of wisdom, my darling mother?"

"I was so hoping you'd ask. I know you're a cautious man and this romance took off at the speed of light. That probably unsettled you."

"It did."

"But you're also a creative man, and that means you have the ability to shift your perception, see things in a different light."

"And?"

"And Molly's a lovely woman and her son is adorable, not to mention he has excellent taste in literature."

"*Taste* being the operative word. He loved chewing on *Ranch Puppy.*"

"Molly and Zack suit you, Bret. And you suit them. Experiencing such strong feelings in a short time *is* unsettling, but that doesn't mean you should run from them. They may be telling you something."

"That I'm an idiot?"

"I'd never say that. I will say that the way you and Molly looked at each other on the sleighride is special. Something that wonderful doesn't come along every day."

"You saw that, huh?"

"I see everything. I'm your—"

"You're my mother and I love you. Thanks for the call."

"I love you, too, son. I'll hang up, now. Go think."

"Yes, ma'am."

34

Molly was looking forward to a quiet Christmas Eve. Tomorrow she'd contact Bret for the first time since that awful parting almost a week ago and ask if she could drive out to bring him his gift. Maybe they could start rebuilding their relationship.

She'd just tucked Zach in when the doorbell chimed. Bret? Heart racing, she held her breath and listened. Nope, not Bret's voice. Similar, but not quite the same.

Creeping out of the bedroom, she peeked down the stairs. Grammy was talking to a tall cowboy but he certainly wasn't Bret. He didn't stand the same way. He'd removed his hat and the light in the foyer picked out red highlights in his hair.

Wait a minute... Gil? She crept down the stairs and her foot hit the one that creaked. The man looked up. Gil.

"Molly?"

"Hi, Gil. What's going on?"

"I'm here on behalf of my brother. If you'd be so kind as to put on your coat and step outside...."

"Step outside?" Her pulse rate jacked up. "Why?"

"You'll see."

Grammy's face was alight with excitement. "Just do it, sweetheart. I have a good feeling about this."

"Okay, Gil. You've aroused my curiosity." She grabbed her coat and he helped her into it.

"You might want to bring a hat, too."

"I have one." She pulled her knit hat out of her trench coat pocket. "Let's see what this mysterious—" She opened the door and gasped. "No way."

"What?" Grammy crowded in next to her. "Woo-hoo! Now that's what I call imaginative!"

Molly rubbed her eyes and looked again. Still there. Parked at the curb and decked out with Christmas lights stood the McLintock sleigh hitched up to Thor. Several neighbors had put on coats and come out to see what would happen next.

The cowboy sitting in it stood and climbed out, his movements heartbreakingly familiar. Bret.

His long strides brought him quickly up to the porch steps. "Miss Molly, can I interest you in a Christmas Eve sleighride down Main Street?" He held out his hand.

"Hang on. I have to get something." She turned and ran upstairs. His scarf wasn't wrapped. Just as well. She rolled it up tightly, shoved it in her pocket and hurried downstairs.

Three faces turned upward at her approach. Grammy had invited Bret inside and shut the door.

"How did you do this? How did you get this sleigh and this huge horse to—"

"That's Gil's and my little secret. Ready?"

"Sort of, but are we going to the Buffalo? Because if we are, I need to change my—"

"No, ma'am." Bret smiled. "Just going for a sleighride."

That smile tugged at her heartstrings. "Alrighty, then."

"Off we go." Gil tipped his hat to Grammy and went out the door.

Bret tipped his hat, too. Then he paused. "Don't wait up, Mrs. J."

"Hey, why shouldn't she wait up? I know a sleigh's slower than a car, but we should still be back in—"

"I think Bret has other plans he's not telling you, sweetheart. Just go. You can't pass up a Christmas Eve ride in a lighted sleigh."

"You're right about that."

Bret put out his hand again and this time she took it. He wasn't wearing gloves and she hadn't put hers on because they were in the pocket of her coat, under the scarf.

Now she was glad she hadn't dug them out. Holding Bret's hand was the best thing that had happened to her all week.

Lacing his fingers through hers, he led her out the door.

Grammy kept it open. She'd grabbed her coat and wrapped it around her shoulders. "I want to see you take off. And hear those bells."

Molly turned back to her. "Thank you for staying with Zach. I wish you could—"

"We'll do this again next Christmas, Mrs. J," Bret said. "There's talk about making it a tradition."

What? Molly looked at him, but he just gave her another one of those million-dollar smiles.

"That would be wonderful, Bret," Grammy called after them.

Molly lowered her voice. "Next Christmas? A tradition? What's going on?"

"I had this idea and now everybody's jumped on it." He crossed the porch and held tight to her hand as they clattered down the steps.

"Are you even allowed to drive this sleigh down Main Street?"

"Absolutely. We still have a few folks who ride horses into town in the summer. Tie 'em up to a parking meter."

"I'm so glad I'm staying so I can see that."

"Oh, you're staying?"

The casual way he said it tipped her off. "You knew."

"Rumors. Small town. Word gets around."

"Did Grammy call you?"

"No, ma'am. Heard it on the grapevine."

Might as well let it go. "Okay, we take a sleigh down Main Street and come back here. Then what?"

"We'll see how it goes."

"That's sufficiently vague. Oh, and please tell me you didn't make Thor pull this sleigh all the way from Rowdy Ranch."

Bret squeezed her hand. "I promise you we did not. He would have refused, anyway."

"I hope you know this stunt makes me question your sanity."

"That makes two of us." He handed her into the sleigh, climbed in after her and adjusted the green lap robe around them.

Gil glanced back from the driver's seat. "Everybody ready?"

"Hit it, bro."

Molly turned toward the house, waved and called out a goodbye to Grammy, who was still standing in the open doorway.

Thor took off at a smart trot, the bells on his harness sounding like echoes from yesteryear, especially since they were on a street, where such things rarely happened anymore. It was a cool effect. But the time and effort required to pull this off boggled her mind.

She turned to Bret, intensely aware of his body heat after several days apart. "I'm not sure what this is all about, but since you're here, I'll give you my Christmas present."

His eyes widened. "You got me a present?"

"I didn't buy it. I made it." She pulled the scarf out of her pocket. "Merry Christmas."

Gil looked over his shoulder. "Nice job, Molly. Very pretty."

"Thanks."

"You made this?" Unrolling it, Bret ran his hand over it. Stroked it again. "When?"

"This week."

"You didn't tell me you know how to knit." He kept touching the scarf, fondling it.

Made her smile. Sensual guy. That's why she'd chosen a soft yarn. "I didn't know how. Colleen taught me. I was at her house getting a lesson when you brought over the luminarias."

"Mrs. J said something about a lesson, but I was so rattled I didn't take it all in. You've been taking lessons from Colleen?"

"Just one, on Monday. After that she coached me over the phone."

"And you came up with this since Monday?"

"I was motivated. And it was fun. Cathartic. Helped me think through some things."

He looked up. "It's beautiful. Thank you."

"Are you going to put it on?"

"I am." He unbuttoned his coat, wrapped the scarf around his neck and buttoned his coat. "It's softer than those socks she made."

"I asked her for something that would feel really good against your skin."

"It does." His eyes darkened. "Not as good as you. But nice."

She peered at him. "You're not planning to seduce me in this sleigh, are you?"

"No, he's not!" Gil sang out. "I didn't sign on for that."

She grinned. "Glad to hear it, Gil."

"On that note, we're almost to Main Street. Time is short, dear brother. Don't you have something you want to say to Miss Molly?"

"Wait." She put a hand on his chest. "Please don't apologize for our last night together. You meant well."

"I wasn't—"

"Before you say anything, let me tell you what I decided while I was knitting your scarf. I'm not only staying in Wagon Train, I'm abandoning Aaron's plan for my future."

"You are? Which part?"

"All of it. He meant well but he's not here and I am. I promised to do something because I felt obligated. But I'm not. It's my life. I'll get married when I'm ready and have a baby when I'm ready. End of story."

"There goes the program, bro. And we're almost to the Buffalo. I'm calling a halt when we get there. Maybe you can still salvage the situation. Whoa, Thor. Easy boy. That's good." The sleigh slid to a stop across from the tavern's entrance.

"What program?" Molly looked over at the Fluffy Buffalo. A McLintock family contingent stood outside holding a sign that read *Say yes, Molly!*

She looked back to the man beside her. "Bret?"

"Molly Dixon, will you marry me?" He pulled something out of his pocket. "I created this from a horseshoe nail, which is symbolic but maybe not as beautiful as a traditional—"

"You want to marry me? But I thought—"

"I was scared. But I'm not, anymore. I know you. I know your heart and you know mine. We belong together, you, me, and Zach. And Zach's little sister."

"His little *sister*? What does that even mean?"

"It means he wants to make babies with you, Molly." Gil swiveled on the seat. "He wants a girl, but everybody knows that's a crapshoot. Even so, he—"

"Shut up, bro. Let me handle this."

"I would, but you're making a hot mess out of it and I—"

"Shut up, Gil." Molly reached up and tugged on his jacket. "Appreciate your input, but Bret's got this."

"I do?" He thumbed back his hat. "Because from my vantage point—"

"Give me that ring." She slid it on her finger. "Fits perfectly." She held it up for him. Then she waved it at the cluster of McLintocks on the sidewalk. "Fits perfectly!"

A cheer went up from the group.

"I'll marry you, Bret McLintock, because I love you so much and I can't wait to get started on Zach's little sister."

"I love you so much, too, Molly Dixon." Cupping her face in both hands, he kissed her.

The crowd on the sidewalk had grown as curious passersby joined in. They made a ruckus, cheering, shouting and whistling.

She barely heard them. She was kissing Bret while sitting in a horse-drawn sleigh on Main

Street on Christmas Eve. A girl couldn't ask for a more romantic moment than that.

Bret deepened the kiss as the crowd went wild. But at last he drew back with a sigh of regret. "We need to change venues."

She gulped for air. "Do you have a plan?"

"Two." He dragged in a breath. "Gil will drop us off at the shop, where my truck is parked. We can either stay there or drive to my place."

"What about the sleigh and Thor?"

"Once we depart the sleigh, my brothers will move in, load Thor in the horse trailer and the sleigh on a flatbed."

"It's good to have brothers."

"Yes, it is. What'll it be? The shop or—"

"The shop. That's where it all began."

He gazed into her eyes. "And where Zach's sister will be conceived."

"You don't know that."

"Yes, I do." He kissed her gently, almost reverently.

When he kissed her with such tenderness, it was like she was a stack of pancakes and someone had poured warm maple syrup over her. The Christmas spirit was wonderful. This was way better.

* * * * *

Things heat up at the Fluffy Buffalo for cowboy Clint McLintock in ROPING THE COWBOY'S HEART, book five in the Rowdy Ranch series!

* * * * *

New York Times bestselling author Vicki Lewis Thompson's love affair with cowboys started with the Lone Ranger, continued through Maverick, and took a turn south of the border with Zorro. She views cowboys as the Western version of knights in shining armor, rugged men who value honor, honesty and hard work. Fortunately for her, she lives in the Arizona desert, where broad-shouldered, lean-hipped cowboys abound. Blessed with such an abundance of inspiration, she only hopes that she can do them justice.

For more information about this prolific author, visit her website and sign up for her newsletter. She loves connecting with readers.

VickiLewisThompson.com

CPSIA information can be obtained
at www.ICGtesting.com
Printed in the USA
LVHW100449141122
732905LV00005B/316